D0993807

THE CUREWIFE

THE CUREWIFE

Claire-Marie Watson

Claire-Marie Watson

Polygon

First published in Great Britain in 2003 by Polygon
an imprint of Birlinn Ltd

West Newington House
10 Newington Road
Edinburgh

www.birlinn.co.uk

Copyright © Claire-Marie Watson, 2003
Reprinted 2003
All rights reserved. No part of this publication may
be reproduced, stored, or transmitted in any form, or
by any means electronic, mechanical or photocopying,
recording or otherwise, without the express written
permission of the publisher.

The right of Claire-Marie Watson to be identified as the author of
this work has been asserted by her in accordance with
the Copyright, Designs and Patents Act 1988

ISBN 0 9544075 4 7

The publishers gratefully acknowledge subsidy from

towards the publication of this volume

British Library Cataloguing-in-Publication Data
A catalogue record for this book is available on request from the
British Library

Typeset by Palimpsest Book Production, Polmont, Stirlingshire
Printed and bound by Antony Rowe Ltd, Chippenham

For Steuart

Acknowledgements

I owe a great debt to the staff of the Local History and Reference sections of Dundee Central Library, Iain Flett of Dundee District Archive and Record Centre, David Stockdale of Dundee Museums and Adrian Zealand of Dundee City Council Arts and Heritage.

I must also thank Moya Fox of Dundee University Library and staff at The National Archives of Scotland.

I can think of no adequate expression of thanks for Tansy Faloon. Her support eased the long gestation of this book. Nicola Wood was a friendly, encouraging and meticulous editor and I greatly appreciate her efforts.

Finally, I must thank my family, for their encouragement and hard work in reading and discussing early drafts.

History is a combination of reality and lies.
The reality of History becomes a lie.
The unreality of the fable becomes the truth.
                                        Jean Cocteau

The Curewife's Line

	The First Mhairi *b.1297*	1297 ~ Battle of Stirling Bridge
Robert the Bruce (1306–29)		1305 ~ Wallace executed
	The First Helen *b.1314*	1314 ~ Battle of Bannockburn
		1320 ~ Declaration of Arbroath
David II (1329–71)	*Davina b.1330*	
		1348–9 ~ Black Death
	Mhairi the Gifted *b.1350*	
		1361 ~ Black Death
Robert II (1371–90)	*Effie b.1380*	
Robert III (1390–1406)	*Helen b.1405*	1406 ~ Pirates kidnap James I
James I (1406–37)	*Grizel b.1420*	
James II (1437–60)	*Helen b.1440*	
James III (1460–88)		1460 ~ Siege of Roxburgh
	Margaret b.1475	

James IV (1488–1513)		
James V (1513–42)	*Grizelda b.1513*	1513 ~ Battle of Flodden
Mary Queen of Scots (1542–67)	*Mhairi b.1540*	1560 ~ Reformation Paliament
		1561 ~ Mary returns from France
James VI (1567–1625)	*Elspeth b.1565*	1565 ~ Mary marries Darnley
		1587 ~ Mary executed
		1603 ~ Union of Crowns
Charles I (1625–49)	*Grissel b.1615*	
		1638 ~ First National Covenant
		1642 ~ English Civil War begins
		1643 ~ Solemn League and Covenant
		1644 ~ Montrose attacks Dundee
	Alexander b.1645	1645 ~ Montrose attacks Dundee
Charles II (1649–85)		1648 ~ Plague in Dundee
		1651 ~ Monck besieges Dundee
		1659 ~ Monck's garrison departs
		1661 ~ Charles' Coronation London

1

I am Grissel Jaffray.

Elspeth was my grandam and she came from Mhairi who came from Grizelda.

I am named for her.

I will write our wisdom here, and the stories of the women who went before and so make a treasure for the women who will come from me.

Elspeth Fraser was born when Mary wed Darnley and when I was small she told me the stories of our women. When I was older I went with her to find the roots and herb and we would dry them. I watched when she tended folk who called for her. And I listened close when she spoke of what ailed them.

This is how the wisdom passed to me.

Twas Elspeth cured young James Fittes of a fever which was like to kill him if the surgeons did not. He was the only son of Margaret Collen, who had thrown many infants before and could not abide to lose him. She saw the surgeons do nothing but hurt and weaken the lad, as they will do, so she sent for Elspeth who was known to the maids of the house.

Tis the nature of curing to match like with like and the fever was terrible so Elspeth must use witch's thimble, which not all may take. It must be rubbed behind the ears before tis given to drink and if the skin grow reddened, it mean twill poison, not cure. Twas said in other times the fairies grew it and if you cut it and were not paid they would not like it.

The flowers must be pounded in a bowl of ivy wood until

the juice run, then put to hot ale and honey and given very often day and night, with a horn spoon, until the fever die. Also let in air, even at night, but when the chills come put hot stones to the feet.

Elspeth stayed with James Fittes five days before the fever died and for many days after until he could leave his bed. She said the Fittes kitchen was a rare sight, so full of strange fruits and much meat, that she could have every day.

When Margaret Collen saw her lad was better she asked Elspeth her price and this was that I should join him at some lessons and take my dinner with him on those days. This the woman agreed and so I am the first of our line who reads and writes.

Elspeth attended her neighbours in illness and travail and in this way kept food on her table, for she was alone. Her man was Robert Jaffray, a seaman. He was killed in the great storm that wrecked the Spanish ships. Some believed God sent it to protect the English Queen but Elspeth said the Devil was protecting his own because she had killed Mary. He lies at sea and died before my father was yet born.

Elspeth was well known at the port and put my father to sea when a place was offered by a skipper in the Flanders trade. My father is also Robert and he have seen many strange things, as seamen will do.

I have no mother. Elspeth tried all she knew but the woman died without seeing me. My father chose ill. He wed a weak and ailing creature who was not from this place, and he did not bring her to Elspeth beforehand.

Elspeth said there is always a price, and this is true.

So Elspeth cared for me as a mother and I grew quickly and strong. When I had learned the wisdom she was minded to seek me a man of substance, so she returned to the Fittes house. But Margaret Collen had died and the lad had been sent away to the Grey Friars College. Elspeth was not welcomed as before and was even called hag, dread name, so she betook herself home and cast about amongst the burgesses of Aberdeen whose wives she had tended.

But again she was misdone.

They have no thought for aught but show such folk. Oft times they will choose not to see those whose skill they once were glad to use. So Elspeth bethought to wed me somewhere else, where she was not known and my health and learning might show to advantage.

My father had been skippering coasters long since so she charged him with discovering a match in Dundee, whence he brought the claret to Aberdeen. He was glad to do it for he too wished me improvement.

After some months he brought home my man, who is James Butchart. He is burgess of Dundee and maltman to trade so Elspeth was willing to agree the match. He did not say overmuch but he was clean and seemed kind, so I consented and we wed at St Nicholas, to show Aberdeen what Elspeth could do.

I wore a new gown of soft stuff that Jessie Donald made. She is seamstress to some fine ladies and dressed me as well as any of them. My man James saw to it Elspeth had silver enough for her.

My cap was finest Flanders linen that Father got for me from another seaman. And it fit close to the ears in the Holland manner. James gave me a ring, got from the best smith of Dundee's Guild and we had good claret and fowls after, that James said was the best feast a man could have, but fitting for the best wife. He is a fine man, my James.

Dundee is a busy place and bigger than Aberdeen I think. Folk here do not speak as I do, though being a port town too, they hear all manner of speech and I can get on well enough with my neighbours. My house be warm and close enough to the malt house for James. I like it fine. The well is not far, though I have had James bring a barrel, for rain be the sweetest water. There is plenty to be had at the markets, though some things be dearer here than in Aberdeen I think.

Hard by the East Port be many crofts and gardens and I have found enough common stuff in the wild edges to keep my herb bags filled. I do not know yet where I will find rarer stuff but I will walk further into the hills soon and can always get Elspeth to send some with Father if I do not find what I need here.

I have begun to make myself known to the women of this place, for I do not wish to sit idle and I am quick about the house. Elspeth told me to always have something of my own by me for though I am from healthy stock, not all men live long and if I am left alone, as she was, I must eat and feed my bairns when they come. Tis slow to start but I am not from this place and there be other women with knowledge here, though many who attend the poorest are no more than ale-sodden sluts I think.

Yesterday James asked why I write in my book and was not best pleased when I said twas for my own pleasure. He said I should take pleasure enough in keeping his house and indeed I do, but it do not fill a day to sweep a floor and shake a palliasse, and I told him so. Then he said books were for noting costs and prices. So I said he might write as much money as he choose, but I would write what please me.

Then I put herrings before him and he said he wanted beef. So I told him to write his beef along with his money and if he did not eat his herring he must sleep hungry. I think he was surprised at how sharp I can be, for he had not seen it before. But then he said my bannocks were very good, so we finished our supper laughing.

I did not like to speak sharp though, for my James is a fine man, and I do care for him, but it pained me that he did not want my herrings. I will ask Margaret Ramsay how Dundee folk make them, though I cannot think there is much to be done with a herring that Aberdeen women do not know.

She live hard by and have two bairns. I gave her dried papple in honey for Lachlan the youngest, for he was coughing much more than he should. He play often in the narrowest closes, as all the wee ones do. Tis because they are full of hideyholes, of course, but the air is not good and when one child sneeze it spread to a hundred.

Margaret have never known how to make cures for she is Dundee as long as she can remember, and none of her folk had the wisdom and knowledge. She have been friendly to me from the first and I am happy to have a smiling face near, for I am yet new here and tis a kindness to welcome a stranger. I would not take payment from Margaret for I think mayhaps her man keep her short, though she be too proud to say. She be too thin, though he look stout enough and I doubt not his fondness for ale.

Elspeth says there is always a price, but I think a friendly word be as good as coin sometimes.

I call this my book though tis no more than loose sheets yet. I have been thinking on how I may keep them good and safe and I believe I will find me a cordiner's needle to stitch them when I have enough for a bundle, then make a sheet from leather scraps to cover the whole. Paper be fell dear but if I write small I need not use too much and I can make a grand dinner out of naught when I like. Also, my name is going abroad, for Dundee folk can chatter like no birds I ever knew. And I have a little purse of my own making.

2

Elspeth's mother was Mhairi, who lived by Fortrose. Our women have travelled far.

Mhairi was thought too crooked and small to live but Grizelda said her bairn was favoured for when she carried her there was the botch in Aberdeen and though none could enter the town, many would leave, for they feared death from its dark lumps.

Now one day Grizelda saw a stranger pass and knew from his dress whence he came, so she took herself to shelter under a big aiten tree.

Our women have ever had a bag full of aiten bark against the botch, for tis a terrible affliction. When it come, neighbour will shun neighbour and the bailies make cruel laws in their great fear of it.

When Mhairi was but six years an Aberdeen man got his face branded with hot iron for hiding his sick child. And Elspeth can remember when they put the gibbets at the bridge and Mercat Cross to hang sick folk who came in to the town. There was one at the shore too, for many ships bring pest. But the bailies also hanged townsfolk who sheltered the sick. And if it was a woman, she was drownded.

Mhairi could not play as other children will do but she was quick of mind and gained the wisdom early at Grizelda's hearth. She feared naught and would gather her plants at night when no-one was abroad, for she did not like the company of others. And it give more power to some plants if they be picked under the moon.

Mhairi was skilled at the brewing and stilling so people would bring their jugs to be filled and this is how she and Grizelda lived until the soldiers came.

There was a wedding in the village and they came by when the dancing was just begun. They had been in Denmark, where many served then, and Mhairi said they were made welcome at first for none would deny them a share in wishing good fortune on a union.

Now, where there is dancing there is always a great thirst and so Mhairi and Grizelda were fairly kept busy fetching as much ale and liquor as the party could drink. But they could not carry more than two jug apiece and so the soldiers, who were thirstier even than the fiddlers, took themselves to the house saying they would bring more. Grizelda did not like it, for they were already loud and unsteady, so she and Mhairi ran alongside and at first they managed to keep them in good humour. But when they reached the house they knocked things about in their haste to find more liquor.

Grizelda thought to give them a quart pot apiece and sit them before the fire, in hopes they would settle and sleep in a short time. And indeed two of them did. But the third had a head like a rock for he took himself another and then began to laugh and make play to catch Mhairi.

She was sharp-witted but slow to move because she was crooked and so when his play chasing turned true he caught her easy and she could do naught against him. Grizelda hit him but he knocked her over and though his two friends struggled awake at the noise, he took Mhairi before they could pull him away.

They ran off all three. Some of the village men gave chase but they were never found.

Elspeth said though she had no father but a runaway bull, and most could not bear the shame of it, she had Mhairi for mother and Grizelda for grandam. And Grizelda said they could hold their heads up proud.

*   *   *

I have found a croft beyond the Dens Burn where the woman, who is Davina, smokes very fine bacon and hams. She have two oaks near her house, so her pigs fatten on the nuts and give sweeter meat than town pigs. She have some knowledge too, for she be a country woman and grow many herbs, but she did not know of the foalfoot. I think she doubted when I told her a root or two hung in the byre will bring a high tide of cream. So I said I would bring her some and if her cow, Jessie, give more cream she will pay me with butter.

Davina be well set, with four fine lads and a bright hearth. I would fain live so, but I know my man must needs stay close to his malting floor.

Most folk here do not walk far from their houses but stay within the walls, yet I like to go out. I think tis because I am in a new place and have not seen it all. And I grew used to walking far out with Elspeth to find our herb. When the days be warm and long tis a fine way to pass a little time. James have said he will take me over the river soon, for I have oft times looked across to Fife and it seem a bonny place. I will make a fresh cheese, which is as easy as sleeping. And if we bring bannocks and a crock of fine ale we will have a dinner fit for any laird. James said it seem a strange thing to do and he did not like to leave his work, but I told him a man with a new wife may do some things he have not done before and he have a good man at the malt house who will mind it for half a day.

There was fighting in the street yesterday. Lads from the Grammar School throwing stones and shouting at the ones from the Music School until the blue coats saw them off. James says they have always done it as far back as any can remember and tis just harmless play acting. I do not think a stone be so harmless if it clout a lad's head and knock him over. And if the dominie clout his backside too he may find other ways to play. I was talking to Margaret Low when the fighting started and she said not long before I came there was a big skirmish when the Rotten Row lads came down to fight the Murray Gait gang. She said they were fined and were lucky not to get a whipping. Lads have no more sense in their heads than young deer, who will butt heads when they have tired of running but do not want rest.

I go to the shore tomorrow for Father may come and if he do I will bring him to the house for his dinner. James said he would get some whisky, for they like each other fine. Twill be the first dinner Father have had in my house and I have a good bit of beef to put before him. I am near jumping to hear of Elspeth and home for she be old now and I fret for her, though she have good neighbours who will make a bit of broth if she be poorly.

I have been thinking on Grizelda, for she it was who made our rhyme. It came into my head not long ago and have stayed there days now. Sometimes a tuneful air will stick like that until another come along.

I will write it here for Father told me Elspeth was forgetting some things now, as the old will do, but is sore affronted that she cannot remember. If I write our rhyme now I may read it when I am old and mazing too. And mayhaps my firstborn lass will add something to it, if she have the rhyming gift, or hers after that. And then it will grow.

> A seed once fell upon the ground
> And from it grew the tree
> Whose leaves do whisper all it know
> And pass but come again.
>
> A woman listened to the sound
> And from her grew our line
> Our wisdom whisper all it know
> And pass but come again.
>
> Her name was lost, wisdom remained
> And from it grew our power
> I am Grizelda. I whisper the power
> And pass but come again.

All our women liked the storifying but none since Grizelda ever had the rhyming skill, that make words roll like pebbles on a shore. Tis a rare gift and make words easy to remember.

When I took my lessons with young Jamie Fittes, his mother told us all about True Thomas the Rhymer, who was Laird of Ercildoune and was gifted Prophecy, Rhyming, Truth and Music by the Fairy Queen.

He said,

> The Burn of Breid
> Shall rin fou reid.

Mistress Fittes said he was foretelling Bannockburn, when the water turned red with English blood.

I told James of Grizelda today for I snared two rabbits out beyond Corbie Law. He said if I was minded to think of family gone before he could think right back to Thomas Butchart, who was a baker like all the family except himself. Seemingly tis written in the locked book that Thomas was made burgess in 1526. James think he bear an old, old name for there are kin who still cry themselves Bouchard. I do not think Thomas be so far back but I said naught for James do not like to be crossed when he talk and his own voice please him better than mine.

And he said my broth was not so tasty as his mother's, though he made to sweeten the words by telling me he liked it fine. Such vexing nonsense. I have told him he will get his favourite dinner tomorrow and he be well pleased for he do not yet know I will make it only very small, then tell him there be no more.

Grizelda was fond of watching wild creatures and when she was yet a lass she saw a hedgehog roll away from his dinner of fermented berries. This put her in mind to set ale mash mixed with a little meal close to a burrow. She sat still as stone until one or two rabbits took it and after small time she had them by the ears and away. She could get birds too, though she took none but the plainest for fear of the laird.

In her time, the laird could cut off a man's hand if he be caught taking fish, fowl or beast from his land. Grizelda said there were some who would even tell the bailies when a man had taken a few rabbits, or a deer, and have him hung for it.

She was born into a land of widows and bairns for James had took all the men of Scotland into England to fight at Flodden Field. They had any horse with a bit of breath left in it and carts and food besides. There was hardly a woman did not curse the English King for taking all they had to give.

3

I have not writ here for so long I near forgot how tis done. There have been much talk about the Covenant made in Edinburgh. Twas bad enough when the King put our ministers in white lace, but now we must have the English prayer book in Scots kirks. All who refuse are punished. Folk talk of naught else just now and none will put up with it. Our ministers would dress in plain black and do not take to a King in London putting all kind of papistry into their kirks so they have signed the Covenant, and all the burgesses, bailies and gentlemen of Dundee have signed it too. I fear they will do the same in Aberdeen and Perth and every other place in this land.

But when the King learn that all of Scotland cross him he will try to hobble us. And war be a King's hobble rope.

James said I should not think of it for tis not women's business. But there is a tale going about that a woman threw her stool at a bishop in St Giles for prating Mass. Seemingly the congregation were behind her for they chased him home with stones.

Tis women's business in Edinburgh.

I have been here many days now and though Elspeth breathe easier I do not think she have much more time left in this world. She sleep most of the day and will take a little meat if I pound it small into her broth, but she cannot sit up for long.

James was sorry to see me go but he found me passage on a

merchantman going to Aberdeen so soon as Father sent word.
I could do naught else, for Elspeth cared for me, so now I will
care for her.

Father be no more use in the house than ever he was. I was
fair sickened when first I came, for the air was foul as a midden.
He thought Elspeth had suffered the ague and bought a cure
from the pothecary, for she was too ill to tell him what should
be done. I sent him out with sharper words than a father deserve
and told him not to return without new bedding and the
makings of a broth.

While he was gone I put water to boil and drew lavender and
aiten berry from my herb bags to throw upon the fire and
sweeten the air. Then I pounded dandelion root and may berries
to mix with the broth, for the first clear the yellow poison and
the second bring strength to the heart.

She grew fair lively tonight. Marjorie Keith came in and took
a cup of the bullister with us. Tis a sweet and warming cure
for all matters of blood in men or women and Elspeth's blood
be thin now.

Marjorie have been a good friend to her since I was a lass.
She brought soft sugar cakes, made with eggs and brambles,
though I know sugar be dread price these days.

She gave us more than she would have herself, for affection
for Elspeth.

They had a rare time speaking of the days when cordials
were made with pot whisky. Tis too hard to get nowadays, for
the excise man have long arms and sharp eyes and he do not
give a body leave to make it. They said Hollands made a good
enough cordial but it tasted better in the old days. The old
remember all food and drink tastier than it could ever be, but
that is a happy thing when they have little else left.

For the bullister take a pint pot of berry and put the same of
sugar, pounded very small like sand, and the same of
Hollands, and stir all well in a crock. Then stop tight with

cork and cloth and leave until Lady Day. It will be sweet and clear then.

Elspeth would have me write the making of the cordial to show Marjorie and they laughed very much that a simple thing to make and tell should look like naught but blades of black grass or curly fern.

Such a fretting there was today for Elspeth's knees pain her greatly, even though she have not left her bed for weeks. I bound them with kale leaves to draw the pain then spoke Grizelda's rhyme, for it soothe her to talk of the women who went before. She wanted to see all the names writ but before I could begin, she said it should not be done. For to make a picture of the names would mayhaps destroy the power and the wisdom. She think our knowledge be stronger if it only be spoken, for then it remain with our women. If it be writ, then all who can read will know it.

But there are so many women in our line it be like a long, long tale with no beginning and no end and it be hard enough for me to remember. If my first lass do not remember all of it then some of our women will get left out when she tell it to her own lass, and that will make the knowledge weaker. I will teach my bairns to read so that my lass will first have the wisdom from my mouth and then from my book. And she will write in it too, and all the women who come after. That will be a fine thing.

Father came yesterday and Elspeth was fair glad to see him. He said she looked very bonny and that made her laugh, though indeed she is yet a fine-looking woman, with good thick hair and some teeth left. He goes to Dundee today and says he will take word of us to my James and bring back word of him. I sent him away with bannocks, for James says none are better than mine and I would not have him forget me.

I do miss him and my house.

Elspeth was cheered very much and though she still do not

leave her bed I think she be stronger. It tire me very much to tend her, for tis not easy to lift even a frail old body many times in a day. But I am glad to do it.

I went to the shore in the forenoon today, for Father be late and the weather have been kind here. The harbourmaster said tis likely his ship was called to Leith. I will wait three days more then go back. If still there be no word, I will send to James to see if he can discover at Dundee where Father's ship lie. I feel great unease but I hide it from Elspeth. She be too weak to fret on such a thing and knows not how many days he have been away.

Tis a week since I put anything in my book and I grow restless now if I pass too long without it. Tis grown a friend to me. Father came early the day before I was to go back to the shore. I saw him far off. Naught but a black mark against the sun. But I knew his gait. Tis strange how this is so and how a step in the dark may be known too. I need not have fretted at all but I was so glad to see him I was near jumping. I would not let him see, though, for he do not like show.

He brought a fine shawl, that James had got for Elspeth, and I was so proud that my man would think to do that. And he sent me a bit of lace for a collar. Now, I know that is very dear for I have only seen it worn by merchants' wives.

He sent no letter but he do not like to write unless it be for his work. Father said he is hale and though he would have me home again, he know how I care for Elspeth.

Truly we had a grand time that night for James also sent money, though I was not short. So I bought two fat fowls and oranges. And Elspeth managed to take near as much as I did. We had Marjorie in too and it was a feast.

Father be away north now so he will not see James to give him our thanks, but I gave him small letter to give to a Dundee skipper. My James is a fine man.

*   *   *

Elspeth would have her herb box down yesterday and looked through all within as though she might use it again. When she had finished, she would have her sneeshing box, that sit tight beside it in the wall by the fire, for the livening of a pinch or two. Then she told me she kept a purse hidden behind them and would have this down too. Also, I must bring her kist and put it on the stool by the bed where she could reach in. So there she sat, with all about her that she ever owned, speaking soft and long on each thing and living again all the times she knew with them.

Her Sunday gown had but two moth holes, for the kist is kept well rubbed with pounded pine needle. I darned them, for Elspeth's eyes see little but inwards now, and then I tried it, turning dexter and about so that she could judge how it sit on me. We laughed, for she was stouter than me when it was made and I must hold it tight at the back with one hand.

After that, she gave me her purse and said it held enough to pay the minister for decent burial.

It must have taken years for her to find that fee and I never knew she did it.

This is the last I write in Aberdeen for tomorrow James take me back. I can scarce form one word but there is naught to be done about it. I cannot sit quiet before the fire nor lie abed for rest. This book is all the comfort I have just now.

Marjorie Keith heard at the fish market that a ship went down with all hands off Wick, so I ran to the harbourmaster for word of Father. He did not yet know and I ran back and forth to the shore with every tide for three days. I said naught to Elspeth and though she knew I was far away in thinking, she slept much and could not muster many questions.

But on the fourth day she sat up, brighter than for a three-week since. When I said I must go out but would fetch Marjorie to sit with her, she looked full into me then said her son would sit with her and that I would see him soon enough. When I returned she was gone.

I sent word to James and he came on the first boat he could. I know he did what must be done at the kirk but to tell truth, I cannot remember much since we buried Elspeth.

He do not speak of the journey home for he fears the sea. I know not why, but so long as I bide with him I know twill not take him, for I am not of water.

Elspeth had me draw one of her whisper stones when I was small. I took the sign of the diamond. The old name do not come to my head just now but I know tis fire. I buried her stones with her, for none may use another's.

I am not content. I do not settle to aught. I draw water from the well and forget I have done it until I go to fetch the bucket and see tis full. I speak to my neighbours as if through a mist, or from behind a wall, though I know they stand clear in front of me. I go roaming far but to no purpose, for I do not seek herb, just the company of the birds that rise far above. I stand on top of the Law and look down upon Dundee as they do and I fear it sometimes, though I know not why. Tis strange to look down upon the ships in the river, so big from the shore yet seeming from there like the craft lads make from leaves.

Father came many times and will never come again.

Elspeth never looked upon this sight, but I know she see it now for I dream of her many nights. James says I toss about and shout in my sleep, and I wake sometimes in great fear, though in the morning I cannot remember what I feared. He says I wake him too and that he cannot attend to his work for it. But I care naught for that. He be further from me just now than a stranger.

Twill all pass when Elspeth settles.

4

The year turns again. Tis strange how time may pass so slow in a day but so quick in the remembering of a year. I have been far north of the town seeking berries, for I am minded to make cordials to honour Elspeth and Father at the New Year.

I went up through Hill Town. I like those folk. The bonnets they make are rare and warm and their market is good, though the bailies do not like it. They hate to see any trade unless it pass across their counting tables. Hill Town folk just laugh at them. But James says twill not be long before Dundee find a way to bring Hill Town and the rest of the lands of Dudhope into the burgh, for tis by controlling trade that the merchants and all other guildsmen prosper and this is why the town be near as important as Edinburgh.

Far out beyond Hill Town lie the hills they call Sidlaws and there is much to be had there in the way of berries and herb. There be bands of rovers too, though many town folk do not like them. Tis only because they do not have town ways and so they are feared, but I like them fine. I have made a friend of one of their women. She must have seen me before I saw her for she surprised me at the chanting of the rhyme.

I was minded to make whisper pieces. Twas the only Margaret of our line who first told about them. She was of fire, like me, and said tis best for fire and air folk to use wood. Earth and water folk must use stone. The best trees are oak or roddin but first you must ask permission of the tree, so you put your hand upon it and say,

Fire, air, water, earth
All are held within
I give you honour with my gift
Pass your secrets in return.

The gift must be salt, and only a small branch may be cut, for there be but twenty-four pieces and they are not large. Burn the marks on them and lay them out under a full moon for a night. At high sun, put them to salt, then through flame and smoke and put water on them after. Then the tree will pass the power.

The rover woman listened when I said the rhyme, then she offered me her knife to cut the branch.

She knew what I did and gifted me wondrous. Twas like meeting a sister, though our lives be so different. They speak amongst themselves in Irish, which is the tongue of the west and the great mountains. But they know Scotch, too, for they make and sell small things for the house wherever they go, and few hereabouts speak other.

I will see them again, though not in Dundee for the woman, who is Morgain, said they would not go near a place of war. We have peace, but the bailies call the rovers vagrant and have driven them from the town many times, so I think this be her war.

Tis a fine thing to find a sister in people who are come from far away and speak in strange tongues, though I would not say this to James for he do not like the rovers. I have even known him to say he do not really like any but Dundee folk. When I said I was not Dundee he said I was different. Then I said the shore be full of folk from other lands and he spend much time down there. But he said that was different too, for they just come and go again.

If a thing do not fit in his mind when he please he will always say tis different. Tis a man's way, I suppose, though it seem like foolishness to me. Tis why I like my book, for it take my words silently, yet I know they please it.

James speak sharp more often than he did before. When I laid my whisper pieces out and heated the poker to mark them he thought I made a game. But when I told him I could use them to see if he be earth, air, fire or water he roared about, getting his hat then said he be none of those, just sore tired of my tormentfulness and thirsted fit to die.

Margaret was like Elspeth, for she had but one son, who was Grizelda's father. She knew much, I think and she gave us more than just the whisper pieces. None was ever so good as her at the bonesetting. Twas said her hands were so quick and sure, none knew what she did until the join was made and the binding done.

And the kine gave her more milk than others could ever get. There was folk envied her for that but they grew to be grateful when she cured every beast in her village.

When the cows began to stagger about shaking their poor heads, folk said they were hag-ridden. Mayhaps someone had not dropped milk and oats on the hillside when they should, but that cannot be known now. So Margaret took a roddin branch, that witches cannot come near, and used it to corner each one. Then she tied poisonberry about its neck to cure it.

James will have to see to the reddsman, for he pay me no heed. Others are putting their soil on our midden to save the redd money but that man just measure the heap and take extra to clear it. He will attend James, though, for he is burgess and could take complaint to the council. Folk are fined heavy if they do not clear their soil but few wish to walk out beyond East Port to the town midden, so many creep to their neighbour's close and leave it there. Some even put it over the wall of the Howff. Tis disgraceful. Though the dead are gone beyond, they are honoured and remembered. Tis why folk pay so dear for decent burial and a fine stone.

The reddsman be charged with walking the burns and wynds to stop such night creeping but there are too many who cannot afford his penny and so would do the work themselves. Or pay another a halfpenny to do it for them. Still, he must garner a fair few pennies for there be none other at the work in this burgh. I surmise he grip tight, though, for his clothes be little more than stinking rags, even on a Sunday. And he do not treat his bound men aright. They are poor, half-starved creatures, dying on their feet. Tis wickedness.

James says it be no more than plain sense to keep men well and fit to work. If it be foolishness to starve a horse so that it weaken and die quickly, then tis the same with a bound man. The council will let no more in to the trade, though I cannot think why. I do not remember Aberdeen so dirty as Dundee, but there is a fresher wind there.

I saw a woman put in the pillory today, and her hair all cut off for adultery. Folk threw mud and horse's muck at her. Some laughed and others shouted and called her hoor but I cannot believe it for she wore a housemaid's clothes. I know well that many work in big houses for naught but board and if it please the master to take them he will, then put them out when all see they are with child. No man would be called fornicator, for the fines are great and he must hang his head in shame before all the town. But the greater the man, the easier it be to fornicate without fine. Great men will always protect one another, for fear folk will think all do what one do.

I have seen it done in Aberdeen before but I never saw such a poor creature as I did today. She was all cut about the face and head, for there were many stones mixed with the muck. Much blood ran into her eyes and mouth. It made my belly roll to see how broken she was. And hear the noise. It must have battered her ears like storm water. I think there are many who carry shameful secrets and great fear of discovery, so they will turn all eyes to another and pray none will look into their own. I could not stay for I was sick with it. But later I went back when I heard the noise stop. The bailies were unlocking the pillory and she looked near dead. I think they feared she might choke upon the neckpiece when she grew too weak to hold her head up.

They put me away when I tried to go near and I was so angered it stuttered my breathing, for I could have tended her.

When I told James he said I had no business tending hoors, for I am burgess wife and he is known to all. I was sharp then, for the remembering of the wickedness I had seen. I asked if he slept in the kirk every week, for I never saw less kindness and charity in any man and few would even do to a dog what was done to that lass. He just said there were too many hoors in this town and none would put up with it. They were like a plague of pox-ridden rats. I told him plain, if Dundee men did not use hoors the town would soon be rid of them.

Well, he roared and raged and told me I was not fit to be heard. But I am no mouse and I do not like roaring in my house. So I roared back that he spoke nonsense.

He do it all the time now. Truly I did not know I had wed such a fool.

Then he said if a man got no peace in his own house he would go out.

I am well pleased to be rid of him. It give me peace to write in my book. I suppose he will take his supper at Jaks but if he do not, he must sleep hungry. He will wake me when he come in. He always do. But I will not get up to feed him.

I went in to Margaret Ramsay after, for I did not want her to think badly of me for the noise. But she just said there was no man born who did not roar at his wife and twas a lucky wife could roar back without getting a black eye for it. I said if James ever blacked my eye he would learn what gelding shears are for. So we had a fine laugh and I played with Robert, her newest bairn. He be sturdy enough now but he was born one of two. They were both tiny and blue but I saw that one might live. So I blew into him first and that was Robert. His brother lived only a few hours but tis a blessing he died then, before she grew to care for him overmuch. She said she was glad to have me tend her and when she asked my father's name I knew she honoured me.

5

We have had the Lady Fair and I had a grand time. Tis the biggest fair of the year and folk come from all over the country, and even abroad, bringing fine things. The town be full, and all are in good humour for there are many entertainments to be had.

I threw horseshoes at the pole but none found it, though James won a penny. He said it showed his hand steadier than mine and we laughed, for he had taken much ale.

The man with the dancing bear was there, who come every year, and there was a group of players all dressed in bright silken stuff like a royal court of olden times. The king and queen wore great shiny crowns and they walked at the head of a long line of actors. All had painted faces and long wigs and they blew horns and sang as they went. Following at the tail were two dwarfs, with a monkey apiece, who ran and jumped and tumbled about until James said he was dizzy looking at them.

We bought fried fish from one stall and hot pies from a baker's lad who ran about with a great tray of them that looked so heavy we could not see his poor legs keeping him up for long. Then I met Netta McFarlane, who live away over by the West Port, and we spoke long for I had not seen her since last Lady Fair.

James soon tired and said he would leave us to our chatter so we passed the rest of the day looking at everything. Netta bought ribbons to put on a bonnet for her lass, who will wed soon. And I bought some dates from a foreigner who come every year with good sweet things. We ate half of them going round, so I must tell James their price was higher than before.

We watched a game of Find the Pea. When the man chose the right cup and won his shilling, I told Netta the next would lose. She asked if I have the sight and I told truth when I said I do not, but I have seen that game in Aberdeen. I told her the man with the cups always bring another with him, who affects to be one of the crowd and then wins money. So the crowd think they may win too, though in truth the man with the cups cannot be beat for his hands move swifter than the eye.

Netta had not seen it done and when she looked close at the cups she was sure she knew which hid the pea but when the next player chose wrong, she said she wondered why I did not play for I knew the secret of the game and would win a shilling. I said none but the man with the cups ever won a shilling and that was the secret of the game.

She would talk about the sight afterwards for Netta do not like silence. Once she get a thought she will talk until day's end about it. She think I am not like other people and I suppose that is truth, for I know more than most about the cures and old tales and suchlike things. But folk with the sight have power beyond mine.

We passed a stall selling eggs and laying fowl. So I told her about the henwives of old, who did not marry but just stayed with their fowl, that gave them more eggs than any other could get. They gave some to the poor and in this way they pleased all mortal men. But some fairies did not like them for it and twas certain they did not please the Devil; all know he do not like to see folk happy.

Henwives knew curing but did not need herb to do it. The touch of their hands was enough. Tis said they had the sight and mayhaps some did, for there are more strange things under the sky than any man may know.

Helen was grandam to Margaret the Bonesetter and she once met a henwife of the old kind who told her she bore a man who would breathe his first when the marked one breathed his last into fire. That henwife spoke truth for soon after the lad was born, word went about the country that the King folk called Fiery Face was killed by one of his own cannon when he put the English from Roxburgh.

Helen lost four infants and that is why she had only one son. But the henwife gave her some eggs and told her if she would have a strong bairn, she must not throw away the shells but pound them into vinegar and drink it. All our women have done that since. Tis why we are stronger than most, I think.

The town have been full of chatter and gossip of war since the General Assembly agreed to stand with the English parliament against the King. It seem the King's ways do not please the English any more than they please us and now we must send an army to England. There have been fighting all over since that Edinburgh Covenant and I have heard it said Aberdeen suffered much for being so prized by both sides. That man they call Montrose took it from the King's men, but then they got it back.

I doubt not my town is full of widows and motherless bairns today.

Now, after all that warring, folk say he be for the King. I cannot put my mind to looking at it. What manner of man would burn and kill while he dither betwixt one side and another? I think he care not which side he stand, so long as it be at the head of an army. When he was true Covenanter, folk said he was a rare leader so I think he changed his colours because he was told he would not get leave to lead all our army, and he would not follow another. It matter not. He have a taste for killing now and I am affrighted.

I spend my days roving far seeking berries and herb, for if there be fighting there will be great need of healing hands. I went to Broughty seeking the foose that cure fire in the body and cool burnt skin.

Long ago our women believed it gave shelter against fire from the sky, but I do not know if they meant cannon, for men make those and only God make the lightning. I hid some snares where I have seen rabbits before but I got naught. I will try again beyond the Hill Town, unless I see sign of the rovers. They would take it amiss, I think. But meat be such a terrible price now I must put some reisted rabbit by if I can.

Folk say our army be the finest in the world, for tis led by Leslie who won a great battle abroad. I do not know why Scots men like to go abroad so much. All my life there have been soldiers going away to fight, for there is a war that will never end somewhere across the sea. Tis a fine thing, I suppose, to have a great army but when I was a girl I saw some of the soldiers come back, all broken like barley after a storm. Folk say the purses are good in foreign armies but silver do not last long in a broken man's pocket.

James says the town must raise a company of men and horses and even give cloth to make soldiers' coats. Men must go whether they will or no and I do not think many are willing. I am too heart sick of all this war-raising to write more. He be away to the watch again tonight.

Each time he go I smile so that if he do not return he will see a bright face with his dying eye. The poor soul have never held more than his malting shovel before and there are few with him whose hands have not grown better fitted to their tools than to a gun. All the powder and guns are put in the windmill by the shore, so I must hope they are given out by one whose hands hold a lamp steady. The council have said that until the present troubles are settled there will be five men to each quarter of the town, with a bailie in charge.

Tis strange they use such a word as troubles when ordinary folk say war. But I have oft thought that ministers and councilmen speak strangely because they write words before they say them.

Ministers use the long bible words to make folk fear sin. And truly some can do it so well, all leave the kirk with the smell of brimstone about their bonnets. Councilmen use short easy ones when they want to make a bad thing sound better. But they like the long words too, for that smell and flavour of the kirk they carry on their backs. They use those when they judge folk, to affright them the more and try to make all men believe they have the right of the matter.

James says the watching is cold, drear work but it must be done or he will be fined. But while he do that he must leave aside his own work and earn naught because of it. And he must pay the levies for the army too. All the folk in Over Gait and Murray Gait must put stones and mortar to fill the gaps in their back dykes, and build all to a good height. If they do not they will be fined.

All this fining. I wonder if councilmen fine their own kind too. Some are put to patching the city wall. The masons will be glad of the work. There be such a terrible rush and hurry about the town now, with all doing what they must to keep it safe. Tis truly a heavy burden we carry.

There was a tun fell from a cart today and it jumped and rolled upon the ground before it stopped at the bottom of the wynd. It must have knocked in the bung when it fell, or else the cooper did not know his business well, for it broke. After all the noise and the shouting of the carter, and the folk running away from the rearing horse, there came a small silence whilst all looked to see what was to do, and if any were knocked over.

Then one saw the hole in the barrel and in a minute there was such a scramble of folk getting pots and jugs and whatever they could find to hold the ale that more were knocked over than the horse had got. Some just lay where they were and supped from the gutter, as though they could not see all the filth it held. The carter tried to push through to stop them but they just roared and laughed and carried on supping, so he took himself back to his cart for fear any would try to push t'other tun from it. He sent a lad for the bailies but when they came they found naught but the empty barrel, and two daft sots who still lay on their faces.

I saw Bessie Stewart knocked down when the horse first reared. Two lads pulled her out of the way and though she will be black and blue she did not break bone. But there was one old soul crushed and he died where he lay. I think he was deaf and did not hear the noise, for he turned too late to get out of the way.

I took Bess home and bound her ankle. She will not walk easy for weeks I think so I will go in and see to her bairns, and making the dinner, until she can manage. She have a lad not yet two years and a lass of four. I would fain have such bairns for both be fine and strong. That lad is never still, sweet lamb. He run about and try to climb up every single thing he see. And he have a smile that would warm the coldest heart.

And that lass. She be the bonniest wee thing. I never saw such curly hair nor brighter eyes. She sat upon her mother's bed, with her legs folded and feet sitting high upon the tops, and would have me guess what manner of creature she made. I could not think and looked to her mother all secret-like, but she did not know. So then the wee thing made a riddle. She said she was a creature, caught by none, that live in the sun. I saw then twas a butterfly.

I never knew the rhyming gift could show so young. She be a clever lass and lit like the sun herself.

6

T is all over the town. Montrose have taken Perth. Dundee be ready for him, James says, and there is no more to be done now but fight the devil if he try to take us. I know he will try. If he can take Perth, he would not wish to leave Dundee alone. There are more at the watch now and a company of Fifers in the town too.

I am as ready for him as I can be. The harvest is in and twas quite a good year so there is enough meal and barley to be had, though we would buy twice as much as the fields could grow, for all are trying to put food by. I know some buy as much as they can carry then send their bairns, one by one, to get more. They sell to others in back closes and garrets at terrible prices. The bailies would set them in the Tolbooth if they could, but so many are at it just now tis like trying to push back the tide.

I have made more herb bags to take what was in Elspeth's box, for I keep my book in there now. I would lose everything before I let it go. Tis like a glass that show me all I am. Foolish fancy. But I become more foolish, I think, because there be so much fear in me. I push it down as far into my belly as it will go, and I keep so busy nowadays I can hardly stay awake for my supper. But I can never lose it.

The war have rattled our gates. Montrose came and set down his camp at the back of the Law, no more than a mile from the town. He sent word that he would speak before setting his men upon us, so Wedderburn and Fletcher went out to him. He told them he would discover the affections of this town, so they answered that Dundee folk had took a covenant to stand against him to the last man. And they said the town was made very strong now.

No man could well doubt this. There are guns all around and about. At Corbie Hill the masons and carpenters have built out flat, to take the biggest. Tis said Montrose took fright at their words for he took his men away and some think he will not return. But this town is a rich prize indeed. He will not leave it be. So long as there is war in this land, twill be fought over as Aberdeen was. And the poor souls bleeding and dying in these streets will not care whether Dundee be for king or kirk.

Some have took fright and run away. James says the council put a warrant out for Lundy. I asked if he left wife and bairns alone here but he did not know.

I dream sometimes how it would be to live in some other place, where there be peace and the wind smell only of sea and clean grass. Though I am town born and bred, I fancy I could fit as well as Davina to a croft, for I have so many tales from our women of beasts and crops I cannot think we would live too poor. But James know only his malting and do not care at all for any but town life. Tis not all men have their names in the great locked book, so he would not stand tall outside Dundee.

And truly he hate it when I show knowledge he do not have. On a croft he would know naught and must become like a child, learning all about the world as if it were new. No, that would not suit my man.

I have read again my fancy of a crofting life and tis like another woman wrote it. All seem ended here, now Montrose have done his filthy business. The ministers say the Devil is everywhere and they are right, for that man was hardly away from Dundee before he was back, with a troop of wild Irish behind him. They burnt Hill Town, as though those bonnet-makers ever did them harm. Truly those Irish are mad dogs.

After, I ran with my healing bags and some food. I took two old shawls and a blanket besides. I thought if folk had naught but blackened stones left for home they would need shelter. Other women did same but what we saw made us stop, for half that town was killed and black. All left alive in it might have been shades. They just stood agape or sat at their doors as though they were the living dead.

We saw old folk that chattered with fear or cold, or both. When we offered our shawls they did not reach for them. Twas as though they had been smited by a great hand and could not move. We saw big hale men whose bairns mewled and pulled at their legs but who could not even turn their heads to comfort them. We saw women with the clothes burnt off them, just sitting in their smoking rags staring at naught.

In all my life my heart never wept so. None of our women ever had healing tales for this. There be no wisdom could say how one man could leave all those folk so handless and witless. Some did not even run so far as beasts from a burning byre.

I liked them fine, those Hill Town folk. They laughed and jested at Dundee bailies. Now they be half gone and I think no bailie in this town would have it so.

James be near deaf with the noise of the guns and though he took no wound at all, he have been shaking very much, and even weeping sometimes. I would kill that Montrose for what he did to my man.

He said none of his watch ever saw such a terrible thing as those King's men, with their eyes all afire and roaring with the joy of killing. Sometimes he sit silent and staring and I know he see naught but the battle. I have no cure for it and he says tis not women's business, but I am in hopes now it may pass soon, for tonight he went out to Jaks as he was used to do when life was still grand.

As if war were not punishment enough for this town, it seem the pest be all about us now. We were to get another company of Fifers but Dundee will not let them in for fear they bring it. If it killed quick and clean, I think it might not be so terrible. But when it come, all are so afeared that neighbour shun neighbour, looking sidewise all the while. It turn good friends into sly strangers, listening out for footsteps on the stair before they leave their house. Folk keep hard to the walls of the close and even if they do speak, tis to say but little, and that with nose and mouth covered up.

The ferry be stopped. Twill not be long before the coalyards are empty. Already the price be half as much again and I have seen women down by the woodyards picking what little scraps they may before the men chase them away.

James do not sell his malt as he was used to do and we are the poorer for it. The inns be empty and tis but a small comfort to have the town quieter for that. Our ships do not leave. Incomers be stopped and their cargoes may not be unloaded, for the pest like nothing better than sailing from abroad. The shoremen have no work, carpenters can get no wood for theirs, and none may send Dundee goods away. All manner of tradesmen must sit at home now, listening to their bairns mewling with hunger.

7

I would kill and kill and kill that Montrose. Did I have him alone for an eye's blink, I would stick a knife under his chin and watch the life bleed out of him like a slaughtered pig. But no slaughterman would kill a pig slow, and I think Aberdeen would thank me for making him wish five hundred times for death before I stuck him true.

Four times he have been there. Tis as though no blood taste so sweet to him as Aberdeen's. And no roasted flesh so sweet as bonnet-makers'. What manner of man would do this?

Tam Kidd got word at the shore and came in to tell me. He think the Four Horsemen must carry Montrose's men, for how else might they move so fast? James chaffed him for it but I would not. Tis hardly a month since first he came. I surmise he misliked Wedderburn's words and punished Aberdeen for Dundee's first thwarting. It seem he went there and put it to the torch. But not before he had left its streets thick-covered with dead. Five hundred are lost in my town.

Tam spoke truth. No mortal man could move hither and yon at such a pace. And no mortal man could kill so many then lay more death at bonnet-makers' hearths.

I could hardly sit still with the fear and raging but James would not stop his boasting of Dundee's great fighting men. I told him Dundee would need great fighting men for if Montrose sup four times at Aberdeen's bleeding cup he will surely come for a second sup at Dundee's. James think this town have beaten him. The man is a fool.

I am so pained with it. It give me such a raging fury I feel tight about the chest and must pound my knees with my fists until it go.

It stop my work. It make me talk out loud to none but myself. James says he is tired of my ranting and would not be with me longer than to sleep. I care not. But I am tired with the rage too, so I will try to think of naught but the women who went before, for they give me ease.

I think of Helen again, for a thought have been trying to sprout in my mind and I do not yet know if I will permit it to grow. It seem too riskful. But no eye will see it writ until the next woman's and so long as I tell her tis the most secret of all our women's secrets, it matter not.

Helen grew very crooked when she was old, and her back bent right over like a bow until she could look only upon the ground. Her legs were knarled too, so she went about with a long pole. She was held in affection, for she had lived so long there were few she had not brought into the world and fewer still she had not laid out to leave it.

The laird of Helen's country was well liked and so was his youngest son. But his first two were idle and feckless. They cared for naught but hunting and would have great sport when their friends came to visit. They were despised for they were once seen tormenting a beast they had brought down. It sickened the man who watched so he ran to put the creature out of its pain. For that they knocked him down and kicked him about the head, laughing all the while. He lay where they left him all the rest of the day until his wife grew fretted. When she found him he was so covered with blood she thought he was dead. But he lived, though he was abed for weeks and was never again the man she wed.

So his wife went to the factor with the tale. He had no greater affection for those lads than any other so he took it, and willing, to his master, though tis no easy thing to tell a man his sons be devils.

After that they were not seen about the country until the next harvest. This time they were not so wild, and word went about that they hunted like gentlemen. So folk grew easier in their minds.

But near the end of the year they came upon Helen, who was out to find whatever she might before all was lost under snow. At first they did but taunt and tease and Helen cared little, for she had seen so many things in her long life twas no more than a puppy's nip to her. She stood and waited until they would tire of her silence, but they did not. After a time, when still she stayed dumb and looking at the ground, as she must, the oldest son grew loud and demanded she look up at him when he spoke to her, for he would be laird when his father passed. He said she insulted him by pretending to bow down with respect where he knew there was none.

Helen said the air grew still and where there had been cruel but harmless jesting there was now a smell of danger. When she told him she could not look up, he gave a great mad shout and jumped off his horse. The other lads were now greatly afeared at his rage and they dismounted, but all slow and silent, watching him all the while to see what he would do next.

He went towards her, speaking soft and slow. The smile in his voice warmed it not at all, only chilled his words so that they dropped like snow from a branch into the silence. He told her if she would not look up at him he must bend far over to look up at her, for surely she thought herself above him. And he did, creeping round and round asking her what she thought he saw when he peered up into her face, and sweeping his hat down low like a courtly knight before a queen.

His brother and the other lads were not easy with it and chaffed to bring him away from his mad caper. Then they spoke serious and warned him to stop. The madman would not listen. His brother put a hand to his arm but he jumped and shook it off, nearly knocking the lad down. He said the old hag would look up at him if twas the last thing she ever did. Then he grabbed Helen's pole and threw it far into the bracken, so that she fell and lay on her side, curled up like new bracken herself.

She was hurt with the fall but angry too and though she

knew she might enrage him further, she closed her eyes and smiled as though she lay in the softest bed, all warm and dreaming of good things.

He could not bear it. She heard him screech and stamp his feet and then she felt his hands close about her ankles. Her poor knarled legs were hoisted up so that her crooked back and head lay flat upon the ground. For a moment, he stopped his screeching and not even a bird could be heard. So she opened her eyes and looked up at him. Then she laughed, full in his face.

Well, his hands fairly flew from her. Twas as though he was burnt. And his face twisted up with fury and hate. He made ready to kick her but his brother and another set upon him and dragged him to his horse, thumping him about the head and shoulders all the while.

They rode off in great haste and discomfort but two lads lingered near. They were afeared great injury had been done and wished to see Helen stand again.

When she was up and leaning against a tree, she sent one off to find her pole and told t'other that if he ran with a mad dog's pack he would get bit. He said he knew that well enough but feared twas his sister would get bit for she was promised and he knew not how it could be undone without great scandal and trouble.

Helen said when the laird heard the tale there would be scandal and trouble enough to keep all the country away from his house and kin. But the lad said though she might try to bring the tale to the laird he would not hear it, for he was ailing now and his son attended to his business.

Helen told him he would hear it from her.

For a day or two there was peace in the village but then the devil came back, making play to be out hunting by himself, but all the while looking for Helen. Folk saw him at the place where he had misused her and because they surmised his intent, they kept on their guard.

But there was one lad out gathering kindling with his father.

He was one of the blessed that never know devices or desires and always tell simple truth. When the laird's son asked him of Helen, the lad told the whole tale, for he could not know caution. So that mad dog smote him. His father found him lying upon the ground with his head on a stone. An innocent killed for no more than the giving of a tale.

Helen was fearsome angered at thinking of all the poor folk in her village who must now live in great fear that their good laird would soon be replaced by his wild son. So she resolved to rid that place of their fear. Folk nowadays would say she did a terrible wrong, but tis our belief she did great good.

When the beeswax had been dripped and melted and hardened, she washed it in whisky three times, softened it again and formed a man and a horse. Then she took tail hairs from the town horse and tied man to beast tight, with one leg strapped beneath the horse's belly.

In the burn that ran by the place where the lad died she found a tiny stone to press into the wax man's head, at the right side by the brow, where the fine flesh sit. Then she lodged her waxens against a big crooked rock that stuck out a little from the foam and went home to wait.

She did not wait long, for not two days later the factor came running to say the laird's son was found drowned in the burn and his horse above him. His foot was caught in the stirrup and his head looked to be knocked against the stones in the water.

8

James be right proud of his sword and have hung it up on the wall. Scrymgeour gave two hundred to Major Ramsay's volunteers. Tis fitting, for folk say the first of his line fought bravely with a crooked sword they called the scrimmager.

We are but two weeks off old Yool. When I was a lass, Aberdeen's Yool mercat was a fine sight, with all the folk crowding to buy fowls and flesh for the feasting, and fruits from abroad. Elspeth always made the grandest dinner she could manage and we took it with strong heather ale. Then she put nuts to the fire and told all manner of tales. Tis sad we may not keep it nowadays. The General Assembly would take all simple pleasure away from folk who need it most particular in times like these. There could be no harm in keeping Yool and Pashe with feasting and merriment, but ministers are a dour lot and folk dare not go against them. But I buy the makings of a Yool board slow and small and we feast quiet at night, when day's work be done. There will be no heather ale this year, for I did not pick the flowers, but I have cordials and I will put nuts to the fire too. Me and James will have the grandest time.

The maltmen are full of ire. Twas agreed at last guild meet they would all go to the council to claim their fee for quartering the troop, but some of them took their swords and turned to riot and the bailies were called. Now the council say they will not pay fees until the maltsters pay their back levies. The levy be greater than the quartering fee so James will not press, but it seem others still have their blood up. I hope they have sense enough to see that losing fee be better than paying levy.

I had took to wondering if I would ever see this day, though none of our women was ever barren. Then I thought mayhaps Dundee air did not suit me and I should have stayed in Aberdeen. But now tis all gladsome. Soon I may put the ring to the thread and see if it turn for man or woman. I must buy soft stuff and make small frocks, and I will knit my fingers off, for my bairn will not come until year end and it must needs be warmer than any other bairn born. James have been strutting about this town like a cockerel since I told him. Tis very good to hold new life in my belly and see it rise upon the trees as well. I look upon a sticky leafbud and think on what wonders there are in the world. And I could jump with the pleasure of it.

Tis hot and the air be thick with dust from old houses getting knocked down. James says tis to stop Montrose's men from hiding in them and to give stone for building up the wall again. There be talk too of digging a ditch by Corbie Hill. He tell me not to fret, for Dundee's fighting men will keep me safe. Such nonsense. Man's work will never stop that devil and his mad horde but I pray mine will.

I was minded to make half a dozen and set them at all the ports and by the shore, but there be too many folk about. So I made only four, each tied to a little gibbet, for I would have that Montrose suffer a noisy shaming death before a cheering crowd.

They sit atop the Law, now. And each one face a compass point, so that no matter where he come from he must look upon it. Montrose will not know he see it, but it will see him.

When I set each into the ground I breathed into it and said it could rest free of its mannikin noose when the man whose image it carried was hooked into his. Then I walked three times around and put salt and water to the ground to finish the work.

None saw me go but tis no matter if they did. I am known

to roam for my herb. This work was never writ before and I asked myself if the writing might not spoil it. But when I looked at my mannikins I knew they would wish to be known for what they will do. I sleep easy now.

Tis dangerous, though. Twas long ago when Helen did her work. Folk reverenced knowledge then. Nowadays there be such a fever for the witch finding, a body may be called witch for no more than foolish argument. They did it in Aberdeen when I was young, after they burnt Marion Hurdie. She called more than a dozen and though some were let out of the Tolbooth after the proving, there was Mallie Cowper and Marion Rodgie left. I suppose they got off with a banishment, for there was not another burning in the town.

Mathow Will's wife told Elspeth she was never so cold nor hungry in her life. She was kept in the dark for days with no clothes, and not given leave to sleep at all. After that she could scarce tell if she were alive or dead. And she said the pricker even stuck his great brass pin into her legs, where they get marked from sitting close to the fire, though any fool would know there be none whose legs do not get blotched that way.

Those prickers.

They say they will find the Devil's mark.

But I think they care less for the Devil than they do for their six shillings a day with meat and wine additional.

Even if a body say she feel the pain of the pin they will not always allow she have no guilt, for if they discover the mark of the Devil's nip they get reward too. Some say tis five pound and more. There are many could find devils in heaven for such reward.

Aberdeen ministers were always terrible keen on the burning. Elspeth said she remembered a time, not long before the turning of the hundred year, when the air was dark and reeking with smoke from the tar barrels. But folk were so well pleased with it the Dean of Guild was commended for his work. I would not be proud of that myself, but it seem there are some in every town with a taste for such horrors.

There were three burnt in Perth not much more than a year past. Tis a fearful business but if I keep well in with my neighbours and give none cause to suspect I do aught but my usual work, there will be no danger to me.

A housemaid knocked at my door yesterday and said her mistress had need of me, so I followed her to one of the big merchant houses off the Over Gait. I have never seen the like. There was a great fireplace in the kitchen and a suckling pig roasted on a spit that turned of itself, though I did not have time to see how this could be done. A fat old woman I took for the cook was shouting at half a dozen lassies, who ran about as though the world would end if they did not get another lippy of vegetables boiled. I would have looked at every pot and crock in that place if I could but the maid hurried.

We went up a back stair and into a room with another great fire in the hearth and a fine big glass hanging over the mantle. There were pictures of people on the walls and brass candle holders. And a gold clock that rang each quarter hour.

The ceiling was a rare thing, so crossed and worked, I never saw the like. There were polished beams with lines of gilded flowers and stars running all their length, and strange birds and fruits painted in the squares between. But of all the wondrous things I saw in that room, the bed was the finest. A great carved thing all hung about with thick red silken stuff.

The mistress of the house lay there upon white bolsters and pillows that looked softer than sea mist. She sent her maid away and would have me sit in a padded chair beside her. But she did not speak for some time, only picked at her fine bedding or passed her fretting hands about her face. I let it be, for I could have sat half the day there. When she did speak at last her voice was too high and sharp and her words fell out all in a rush. She told me her lass had need of me but I must promise never to speak of what I did for her. I could not think why she would lie abed if twas her daughter who ailed but I said I hold secrets close. Then she huffed and sighed and passed her hands over her brow again and again. I told her she did not seem well but she just put a shaking hand to a little bell that sat on a table by the bed amidst a great clutter of pothecary bottles. When her maid came back into the room she told her to take me to the lass and bring me back when I had done.

So we went up another back stair and along a passage all laid with rugs and into another room, not so grand as the first but fine enough and with another fire in the hearth. I cannot think where they find so much coal in these hard times.

The lass was sitting by a window and though she was not more than fifteen years she had the grand manners of one twice her age. She had me sit down and began to ask what I do and where I live, going all round and about without speaking at all of any ailment. I soon grew tired of the game and told her if she did not tell me what ailed her I must leave to attend to my man.

She looked out of the window for a small time then turned back to face me and said she believed she was newly with child. But she was promised to wed the son of a great man outwith this town. She would not say who. There was to be a fine gathering in the house that night to celebrate the match. Though she would not wed until she attained sixteen years, the lad was called to the war and both families would have it settled now.

I asked if she would have me attend her until the bairn came. She looked out the window again then said she had it from her mother that women such as me had ways to right past wrongs and misdeeds. She would not let a great misdeed spoil a good match and a life away from Dundee.

I am too clever to be trapped by such women as these into doing what would hang me so I told her I must needs speak to her mother and would return. I never saw such a cold creature and I did not like her, but when I looked about that house, I saw that my price could be what I made it. I knew I must think slow and careful and go down every imagining of those women's minds, so that when they put their wits to mine I could see the end of their path before they had found it themselves.

When I went back into the first chamber, the mistress was like another woman. She sat upon a chair by the fire, with her hair dressed and a loose, rich gown wrapped thick about her. Twas made of so much stuff it fell about the floor like a river. She held wine and offered me some so I took it, for I would have my small share of her fine and easy life. Then I saw the dark, wet look in her eyes that told what all her pothecary bottles held.

So I smiled at her broad, for while she was that way I knew she would speak of herself with pleasure if I did but flatter, and I might sit and sip wine a little longer. I told her I had seen no house finer than hers in Dundee, which is no lie for I have walked every gait and wynd in this town and none ever stopped me from looking at a grand house as I did it.

But she heard what she wished in my words and did speak for two glasses more about pattern books her man had brought in from abroad so that they might have their chairs and such fashioned in fine foreign manner. A chair be naught but a chair and she take enough wine and potions to make even a plain stool seem feather padded, but I made my eyes wide at the tale and she was well pleased.

She showed me a device she said had come from Italy. A pierced and decorated contrivance to hold herb against the pest. Any man would be proud to say he had made such a thing, for twas truly beautiful. But when I asked her what she put in it, the fool said only 'sweet herb'. I looked within and saw no aiten at all so tis sure she be duped, as all rich folk are, by a pretty thing that hold no goodness.

She asked what might be done for her daughter's ailment, as though we did not both know twas no such thing, so I frowned and said I must needs think hard on what was best to do for such a poorly lass. She asked how long I might be in the thinking and preparing a cure so I told her I would return in seven days.

She misliked my words. Stood up and said it must be done at once. That she would have me back in three days, when her man would be away. But I will not be spoken to thus, so I stared hard at those black shiny eyes and told her she might get a pothecary to attend the lass if she wished but that I would return in seven days. Then I turned my back and left her standing there.

She will do my bidding.

9

I know not what Dundee folk can ever have done to draw such terrible things upon the town. My work did not keep the beast out. He sent a man galloping through the West Port, who blew on a horn and shouted he would see the Provost with a message from Montrose. I saw him pass for I had been at the Friars Port getting new oak leaf from the fine tree that grow near there. Folk stopped and stared. Then a man ran through into Over Gait from Corbie Hill shouting to ring the bells.

Ring the bells, he said. Over and over. And it seemed none could move for a long time. But then a lad turned about and ran like a hare to the Old Steeple.

Andro Barr the locksmith said after that Montrose would have us give the town over to him. But the Provost would not. He had that messenger set in the Tolbooth and Andro put to mind him. The man told him Dundee must give in, for Montrose had a great horde at the Play Field and another running eastwards along by the Scouring Burn, that could come in any port and take the town easy. Andro told him Dundee men would beat the likes of him with one hand and one eye, but he had wit enough to tell the bailies all the man had said, so we would be ready.

All the time the bells rang and rang and men were running to the windmill for guns, then running back to take their posts around the wall and at the ports. Major Ramsay's men came from all over the town to get the boxes of powder and shot up to the big guns at Corbie Law. Where there had been just folk going about their work, it seemed all on a sudden every man in the town was out and shouting to his fellows to get out of his road as they crossed each other and jostled, tripping over their own feet or their long leather aprons.

I tried to look for James among them then bethought me to go down to the windmill, where he must go to get his gun. I was minded to run out by St Nicholas Craig beyond it and try to get away along the shore. But it took a long time to get out of Friars Wynd, for the press of men running to the port, and women and bairns scattering and screaming to get off the street.

When I tried to get over to Cowtie's Wynd and down to the river, I must jump to one side then t'other to keep out of the way of all the folk. I was pushed back by a line of men running up from the windmill. But I shoved harder and cried loud all the while asking if any had seen my James.

One man shouted at me to get away home, but I could not turn round and must run along among them until another shoved me aside and into the line running up into the town. I faced the wrong way and lost my footing. I would have been trampled had not two men turned me about. They held my arms, shouting all the while that I was a stupid woman and should keep out of their road. They would not listen when I shouted back that I sought my James. I was carried along Nether Gait before they let me go.

And then I thought I must surely die, for the big guns started. Montrose did not wait long for answer. When he saw his man did not return, he sent his demons running in across the digging and over the wall, then up the Corbie Law and on to the new-built flat. Folk said they came screeching like a river of mad, wild devils. I think none will ever chaff Tam Kidd again.

They ran so tight together they might have been one. Our poor men tried their best but we needed the troop that was long gone. No man could have worked the guns fast enough to stop them. They swarmed up the hill like a roaring tide and our men fell like standing oat before the scythe. They took our guns and just turned them about. Fired them on the town until folk were half deaf with the noise of it. Cannon ball was the first. It broke through roofs and chimneys, setting loose the fires within the houses. I could feel the ground shake, and glass flew out of windows. Some buildings crumbled like dry bannock when a ball fell in front and each time one fell, twas like a pebble throwed into the sea, that make a ring of foam rise up to the air above. But twas no foam that rose after the ball landed for they threw up mud and stone. And where they fell upon a body, there was bits of it mixed in with the mud.

The smell of it was like having nose and mouth filled with smoking pennies. I have not lost it yet and I think I never will. There never was such sharp unnatural stink as that Montrose spread.

Tis said he stood up there, still as stone, just watching. When his cannon ball were done he put his hellhounds to firing all manner of broken metal rubbish. There was small bits of chain and rusty nails all packed in tight to the gun mouths. That hard mix flew out very wide, but it did not kill quick and clean like ball. One gun could send hundreds of hot, sharp teeth screaming and raging about. Even the smallest piece could take off half a face or scour the flesh from a leg, and what it left looked too torn ever to mend. The noise of that shot was bad enough but there was worse screaming from the tattered mouths that lay dying. None could get near to stop their pain with a merciful sword to the neck.

None of it were enough for Montrose, though. When he saw the first part of his filth was spread, he sent more of his madmen to break through our gates and burst like a hellish flood upon Dundee. They took the Mercat Cross. They even took St Mary's. Half the town was burning. Folk were falling over the dead and bleeding. Others ran hither and yon trying to find escape, though there was no safe place. Bairns were knocked over and trampled into bloody mush while their mothers ran screaming back and forth seeking what could never be recovered. There were dogs and cats and pigs running about, mad with fear of the noise and the fire.

Horses too and even half a dozen cattle that broke loose from the shambles and knocked folk over in their thundering haste to get away.

When the guns stopped and I could come back into myself, I could think of naught but getting back to my house, so I crept eastwards again but must keep stopping all the while, trying to still my trembling legs. Folk were running up closes and huddling under stairs as far from the road as they could. I followed, but each time I would try to creep into a covered place twas full and none in it could move a limb, so tight-packed were they. None could go out the backs of the closes for fear those madmen would come across the meadowlands too. So folk ran up the stairs and were banging on doors to be let in. But then others would be trying to run down the stairs and out to look for bairns and such, so there was a terrible pressing and huddling there too. I made little way and ended pressed hard against a close wall, back across near Friars Wynd, but hard by the street, with a small bairn holding tight about my knees and her face buried in my dress.

Then I saw those red-haired Irish running down into the town from eastwards, all screaming and roaring. They broke open the luckenbooths and swept all from the boards as they went. I saw two stop at a close just across the way and they took one poor soul out, praying for his life. I took him to be advocate or some such from his dress. They pulled all the clothes off him, even his shoes. Then they ran him through with their swords and left him dying there in nakedness that would have shamed him. Others followed and they laughed and kicked him where he lay.

In my close we watched that man die and could not move nor hardly even breathe for fear the same would be done to us. I have heard since they did same to any man they saw who wore a decent coat. They would kill a walking man but would not stop to finish the slow dying who lay about the streets all broke and wheezing as they bled and cried for their mothers.

They thumped in the door of the inn further up and we

could hear them breaking bottles in their hurry to steal all it held. Some ran out with kegs but others stayed where they were and drank and roared until that place was dry.

Twas long before they passed and I waited until the noise seemed far and faint, then made bold to take a swift look up and down the road. I saw no soldiers and bethought me to run across to my wynd and up the stairs to home, if any home were left.

But then I heard them coming in again from east and west, so I drew back so far as I could and whispered to an old man standing behind me that if they were intent on breaking and stealing all they could find at the inns, twould not be long before they took into their heads to seek out more liquor from the depots near the shore, or the cellars of any fine-looking house not burning. If we stayed in the close they might find us and if the wind changed, it might blow fire from a burning roof to ours. He said he had been putting his mind to the best thing to do and if we could creep out the back and reach the Howff we might keep far enough away from the burning and the soldiers to stay alive.

I could see the sense of it but there must have been two dozen folk standing in our close and I could not see how so many could creep quiet and unseen. He said we must go light-footed, holding close to walls, as fast as we may, two or three at once and leaving a little distance between. In that fashion it might be done. Then he said if any saw or heard Montrose's men they must fall to the ground and make pretence to be dead. None must show rings or baubles for the soldiers would seek these as booty and cut off a finger if a ring did not slide off easy. I shoved my ring into my hair so far as it would go, and fastened my cap on tight for fear of losing it.

Then the old man told me to push down one side of the close and whisper to all the folk there and he would do same on t'other. I was to seek out any I saw who might seem to have wits enough to lead two others and drop down flat if needs must. And I was to discover whether any carried meat or fowls from the morning's marketing. If none did, I must seek out any hen or even rat I could find when I got to the yard at the back of the close, alive or dead it mattered not, and bring all back to him. I told him if he was minded to cook dinners when we got to the Howff the fire would be seen plain by any who cared to look and we would be undone. But he said twas not for eating but to have the gizzards to spread thick over hands and faces so that if we must fall to the ground a soldier would believe the better that we were dead.

There was a woman with a tiny babe and two small bairns who clung to her skirts and though she was greatly afeared, she listened well to the old man's plan and said she would be out of that close so soon as she might if twould keep them safe. She said her bairns would do her bidding and mayhaps if others saw them seeming fearless they would follow, and older folk with them.

She began to pass the word with me. There was a very old pair who said they would not go, for if they must fall down they would never get up again and they did not want to cause the rest to slow. But the wife had a fowl and she gave this to me.

They were fine brave people and I wish I knew whether they lived or no.

At the end, twas the only fowl we got, but there was a lad said he had a good knife and a fine sure hand for throwing it so he would get us a rat apiece if we would have it. The old man told him if he got three brace before the counting of a hundred he would give him a penny a tail, and the same again if he would gut them and spread himself first with gore to show the other bairns twas naught to fear.

I never saw such a smile as that lad gave when he pushed back through with six monstrous things. He said the fires were making rivers of rats run out and seemed well pleased, though none shared his joy, for what creature is hated more? The wee lass that clung to me would not dip her hands into the ratgut but then the lad, Wull Greig his name was, came up and gave her his great smile. Once he had took her hand in his thick-blooded one, she let him guide her.

So that was how we were when we crept out the back of the close, the woman and her bairns first, with a man behind, creeping along the walls then crouching low when we must cross the bushy lands at the edge of Tenters Hill. The wall was breached in half a dozen places and though some folk had trouble getting over, and all ended with cut hands and torn clothes, we passed into the Howff without once seeing a Montrose man. At the first, all huddled together but the old man said we must keep in twos and threes and lie down close to the stones. And he would have us spread as much mud and leaves as we could find on our clothes for better concealment.

We lay there with faces turned to the earth like dead things until the gloaming fell. We could hear the drunken singing and shouting and the roaring of the fires that would leave us all without a roof.

Terrible burning lit the sky but it did not warm us all that long night. The wee lass who was with me was froze. She said she was Annie and knew not where her folk were now. She shivered all the time for her frock was but thin, so I tried to warm her by setting her between me and two young lads and wrapping her tight in my shawl. Mayhaps the bairns slept but I did not. I feared for the life I carry. I was too cold and the ground was hard and lumpy and wet, so the marrow iced in my bones. We could hear shouting and crashing but the noise grew less as the night passed. I suppose those drunken dogs took their fill then slept where they fell or went back to the Play Field.

I thought on my James and wondered if he still lived. I thought on how I might heal him if he had been torn by those hellish cannon teeth. Then I thought upon my house and tried not to pray twas untouched by fire, for I surmised twould be better to think of it gone now than hope in vain. I could feel the ratgut and mud stiffen on my face and hands. The stink and taste of it put me in mind of the graves upon which we sheltered. I wondered how long we must lie here, and what Montrose's men would do when light came. I wondered what was left of Dundee, how any would find shelter if the fire took all the town.

When the first bird called I looked up and saw that thinning of the dark that betoken light to come. I could feel the bairns' breathing quicken at the sound and told them they must keep still again, though they knew it well before I said it.

When the first shapes could be seen we heard a horn and then the thundering of horse and more screaming of men. At first we bethought it Montrose, returned to fire what was left of the town. But then one lad looked up above the Howff wall and said he saw Irish fleeing from troop with many horse and standards. He would stand and cheer but was pulled down and we lay until the morning was half gone, for fear of more shooting and killing.

Then the bells rang again. A tuneful peal. Some rose and made to venture back into the town, but still creeping and ready to drop if the tide turned again. I knew not what to think of the new ringing but I feared Montrose had not left, and that mayhaps he played a tricky game with us. I did not want to go near but could not see how I could spend another night in the cold. I was frozen and hungry and so thirsted I could hardly speak. And the bairns were girning and jinking all the time with the hunger and cold, so we crept back to our close. Then one of the lads looked out to the Over Gait and said he saw a man he thought was Provost marching at the head of others to the Mercat Cross.

Well, we fairly ran along to hear what was to do. Folk stood back from us and I know now twas because we were all mudded and gory, but we had forgot. Fires still raged and I could see flame and smoke pouring from buildings by the Kirk Yeard but I could think of naught but the warmth they gave and the hope that the Provost would say Montrose was put out of the town.

He shouted that the enemy did flee for their lives before the mighty sword of God and General Baillie. And that in upholding the ways of righteousness, Dundee's fearless men had rid the town of the Antichrist.

He said Dundee folk should be proud to have stood fast against all evil and though some damage was done to the town, we would rebuild even stronger than before. I looked about me and saw a poor, broken place. The streets were thick with all manner of pitiful carcass of man and beast and there were other pieces so small and bloodied none could know what they had been. Some buildings were burnt to the ground and others still smoked. The Old Steeple stand crippled now, for the church that formed its hem be ruined. Twould make the Lord weep. There were great holes all over the road and a stink of roasted flesh and soot and wet wood over all the town. I do not think I would say only some damage was done, but mayhaps the Provost have seen worse.

He said the General had left a troop of men and horse to keep Dundee safe and had gone to finish his valiant work. He said Montrose would be captured before nightfall. He spoke nonsense, tis sure, for I know now that naught will kill that hellish thing. He was not even hindered by the old, secret ways.

The Provost asked for all willing hands to help the General's men in passing buckets of water to the fires and taking the dead into St Mary's, so that all might come and see if one of their own lay there. We stood a little time first, to make faretheewell, as though we were family who must take leave of each other forever. Twas a very strange thing.

The old man took my hand and said I was a fine woman. I had not asked his name until then, yet he had kept us all safe. He said he was William Russell and when he was young he had gone away soldiering for a foreigner and that was how he learned all the ways of the warring game. He said Adolphus who trained him was the finest man who ever led troop. I said I thought Russell the finest man who ever led folk and we laughed and laughed so hard that others round about started too. Twas fine. Then we said each to the other where we lived so that if any got home and found naught left they might go to another's house for shelter.

Annie was for no more talking of foreigners but would run back to see what was become of her folk. The lad the same. But I held both tight for a time until they gave me promise they would seek me out if aught was amiss, and come in to sit with me sometimes after, even if all was well. When I let go, they were off like rabbits before a dog. I think they will be comfort to each other if needs be.

Even after all had gone their ways I still stood, for I pictured my home as I had left it and wished for naught more than to be supping broth at my own hearth with James, and all the town fine and quiet as before. But I did dither and dally about for fear of finding all destroyed there as twas in the street. At the end of it I went up the end of Market Gait and just walked in the burn. I had a fancy twould be better to face a ruined house if I was clean of all the muck that lay upon me. There was an east wind still blowing, the worst and coldest in this windy town. I scarce felt it. I just stood with the water pulling at my feet until I sat on a stone, holding tight with one hand, for the burn rushed down and I feared to be taken with it.

My robe was soaked and muddy and clung cold to my legs. But I just lifted wet hands to my face over and over. Then I took a fancy to stick my whole head in and had my cap off before I was minded to think on my ring. I picked and poked and at first could not feel it. Then when I did, my fingers were so froze I fretted I would lose it. But it sit on my finger now and shine like a glad memory of happy times.

I do not recall how long I sat there before I heard a flesher shout to me to get out unless I would live through fire to die in water. I did as he bid, but so slow. Like an old, old woman. Then I went back to see what was left of my house.

I felt no cold nor wet until I got to Sea Gait and saw all the houses yet stood. The cannon had not hit the East end of the town, though to north and south was smoking roofs and holes where windows once were. And the wind had took all fire away from us and over to Kirk Yeard.

When I got back to my hearth at last I saw more folk than ever filled my room before. I knew not who they were and mayhaps some were without roof, but I was too cold and tired to ask. One woman had used some of my reisting in a broth and offered it to me as though she sat in her own house. There was three sitting on my kist and twas then I thought on my book so I shouted at them to get up and fair scrambled under petticoats and Sunday garb until I felt its leathern wrapper safe. I said no more but pulled out dry linen and Elspeth's old gown and told all to go out and wait on the stairs until I put them on. They would have sat long by my small fire but I shouted again until they moved.

When the door was shut, I looked again in the kist. All was sooted, right to the bottom, but naught was harmed. I could not think why I should be so spared and other folk not. Then I opened my door and brought two poor souls in again. The rest had gone.

I saw from their dress they were fisher women from Broughty. They had just set their baskets down when the guns started so they had done as I did, running in and out of closes until they came to mine and followed other folk up the stairs and into the house. They said the other folk were Dundee and were gone to see what was to do at their own places. But the women would not go until they had gave me thanks for the shelter they found in my house.

They said a man had run in not long before, shouting that he sought Grissel and if any such were to come to the house they were to say he was away to see if his maltings still stood. I must sit down then, for my legs would not hold me, so glad was I that my James was alive. The women gave me what broth was left and sat until I had finished it.

When they were gone, I looked about me and saw all my house as I had left it only the morning before, though now thick-covered in soot. I was so tired I wished for naught but to sleep for a week but I would have something to set before James when he came in so I put porridge to the fire and cut my wet gown up into cleaning rags. Twas a terrible waste but I would never wish to wear it again.

He ran up the stair like a man half his age, not broken and silent as before but bright eyed and breathing hard as though he had put a penny on a scrawny cock and left the fight with a shilling. He did not shout so loud this time, for at the first firing his watch had stopped their ears with bits of lint, but I saw his sleeve blood-soaked. His arm was hit by a piece of broken chain that had gone right through another man's neck before settling in the soft flesh above his elbow. But he had pulled the piece out easy and kept it as talisman against ill fortune. I could not see that fortune favoured us but each have different fancy and I know James be more favoured than the poor soul whose neck took the broken link first.

The surgeon to his watch was Morrison from Murray Gait and he had done a good enough job. I took the binding off and the wound seemed clean, but still I put ivy and honey poulticing to speed the healing. I have watched close every day since, in case he take a fever from poisoned blood but the wound seem to heal clean.

He would not stay long after. Just supped his porridge like a starving man, then said he must be off again to his work, for there was not a drop of ale to be found in the town. And he must take his turn at the watch again after. I asked who was left alive to watch but he shouted he could not fight and count the dead at same time.

Tis sure he will have fewer friends to meet at Jaks now.

10

This war have cost far too dear. We paid for the keeping of the troop yet there was none here when the blow fell. Now we must quarter and feed Baillie's men and animals, though so much food and fodder was lost in the firing we can scarce feed ourselves. I lie abed sleepless some nights.

Montrose was sighted not far to the north.

I fear for the new life I hold and would run far if I could but there is nowhere to go. The pest be all around us now and it cannot be long before it come in to Dundee. Folk say tis at Meigle and Perth, so it matter not whether he come from northward or westward. He will bring it.

I tried to go up the Law today to see what became of my mannikins. But there were soldiers and I think they thought me strange when I said I came only for the smell of clean air. They are quartered at Dudhope's Castle and even if none stand watch on the hill, others will see me climb, so I must await their leaving, if this war ever end.

I have thought long on why the mannikins did not stop Montrose and it came to me last night that mayhaps they bide their time.

Many of the horde ran off with him but there be a pit full of the limed carcasses he left behind. James says some were those highland folk who hold only to the law of their own kin and care not for our ways. They are like cousin to McColl's Irish, speaking their tongue and bringing their women and bairns with them to the fighting. They followed him far and tis sure he must avenge them. If he do not, their kin will turn on him, for he is not of their breed.

Mayhaps the women and bairns have spoke to the mannikins from the pit and would see an end to Montrose themselves. For though they must love war to follow it all over this land, if some fall at every battle their breed will soon die and I think not even those strange wild women would follow a war-maker to such an end.

I went back to the merchant house on the day appointed, though this town be all so changed it might be ten year since last I sat with that rich, ruined woman.

I have her now, ready to do aught I may bid.

When first I knew what she was pleased to lean upon I picked me enough of the dwale to brew a jug full, for I was minded then to take her pothecary's shilling if I could and there are bushes that grow wild in all corners of the crofts round about.

I found her abed again and looking right poorly. She tossed about, but feebly, and was wet with sweat. All the bottles on the table by her side were empty so I asked if her maid would not fetch the pothecary to her. But the maid was gone, she knew not where, and she could send no other from the house. Her mouth would not form the words aright. So I took the bottles and told her to bide short time until I could bring her cure.

Tis truly a stroke of fortune for me, for I have not only my jug full, but pothecary bottles enough to sell that woman and all like her as much as I will. When I returned, I told her the pothecary shop was all burnt out but I had made better cure myself. I spoke truth, but she heard naught but cure.

She could not even take it herself at first, and I must hold the glass for her.

As I sat by that rich bed watching the woman gulp and gabble her nonsense, I thought on how I was looked at strange when first I came in the kitchen door.

I misliked it.

I surmise there be two sides in that kitchen and most are for the master.

If the housemaid have run away and the mistress have none to trust but me now, I must bring the master's people over to my side before I may set my feet well under the table. I must think on how best it should be done, for those folk say little to me, except for the cook, who be sharp as an old hen and twice as quick to nip.

Twill be best to learn what ail each in the house and cure it quicker and better than they may themselves. I must watch to see who go to the luckenbooths and listen close to what other folk have to say about them. Tis no easy thing, with sharp wits all about, but Dundee folk do love to talk and my wits be sharper than most, so twill not be long before I may come and go as I please.

But I must watch that cook close.

When the woman was quiet I asked about her lass, for naught had yet been said of her. At last she brought her mind back to it and sent me to the girl. I had thought long on what had been asked of me, most particular because of the life I carry now. But at the end of it, I thought that life worth more than any other and if a merchant daughter did not care for what she carried, twas no business of mine. Mayhaps another curewife might get the girl to bed and feed her the potion, then attend until the deed were done. But I was minded to do different, for I would not risk anything for such folk. So when I went to the girl's chamber twas with naught more than the aiten berries in my hand.

I thought to leave them with her, tell her how they might be prepared in different ways for different purpose. I thought to say mayhaps the fear of the cannon fire and fighting in the street had lost her the babe already but that she would know better than any whether she had need of the berry or no. I had the words all said in my head first, so that I might give them quick and without a stumble and then leave before she could say aught in return.

She took them silently, looking upon me with hatred. But I saw fear in her glance and so I told her twas best if the preparation was done fresh and by her own hand, so that no other might see. Then I said she might call another to the house if she would, but that I knew of none in this town of gossip-mongers who would hold her secret closer than me.

When I left, I said I would be attending upon her mother below but would come to her so soon as she might call.

In this fashion I passed two of the warmest nights I ever had and fed finer than I think I shall again.

The servants and kitchen folk were not right pleased at first. When I said I must order up broths and meats for the better curing of their mistress and her lass, and had need of them myself besides if I was to watch aright, they sent up a manservant to question the mistress. He would have me leave the room while he did it but I said I would not move until I saw them bring such food as I bid for the poor ailing souls. I stared hard at him all the while and saw him mislike it. But when the mistress nodded, he obeyed.

After he left the chamber, she moved slow from the bed to her chair and had me brush out her hair. I never saw such a feeble creature. She would not even lift a brush. But tis none of my affair and will all make for the better showing of my skills if she need me more each day and tell her servants so.

When she was settled, I asked why her serving people seemed so sharp to me, and if she never ventured to order them to do her bidding. I told her I could not attend her or her daughter aright if I must struggle to get what I want from them. But she said she had come to the house new wed and the kitchen and serving folk was all her man's. She had lost the only one that ever had a care for her, that maid who ran when Montrose came.

I took a sharp pain of sorrow then, for though she have every fine thing a body could wish for, I know now she be so alone she must make believe a maid was true company.

After she slept, I went up to see what was to do with the lass.

She had not called me but I knew I could not leave her alone when the aiten berry began its work. All the house seemed quiet but when I got to the door of her room I heard a man's voice, though I could not hear what was said. I was turning to go back down, thinking to come again later, when the door opened and a fine-looking man came out. He looked at me long, then asked my name and when I told him, he said I must go in to his daughter soon, but he would speak to me first.

He took me back down and along to a room with more books than I ever knew there could be in the world. They was all fine-set against the walls. Line upon line right up to the ceiling. And all agleam from the bindings and goldenings and such.

I saw from his dress and manner he must be master of the house but I did not know what I might rightly say, for mayhaps he knew not the true condition of his lass.

He smiled, and his words sounded right courteous and even kindly, but his eyes stared into me as he spoke so that I could believe he knew my every thought. I was afeared, though naught he said was other than gentle. So I gave him back a good stare until I could collect my wits.

He just smiled the more and asked about me and my James. Said he knew Aberdeen well and thought it a very fine place. I could not see why he would pass time in this way but his look held me all the while so that in answering all he asked, I forgot the lass, until he told me to go back to her. Then he said I must come back when I heard the knock in the morning, for he would speak to me again.

The night passed easier than I thought it might, though tis sure the lass did not think so. She will learn in time, if she be lucky. The aiten do good work but sometimes the berries make all barren where they pass. She must be steady as the moon, forbye, for there was naught but a bit of gore to be seen on the sheets and there are many her age would never know aught was amiss until three moons had passed. Though she was happy enough to have me there in the night, when all was done, she would treat me as serving maid again, telling me where to find clean linen and suchlike and bidding me be rid of the old.

Her manner was no better than before, but I would keep well in at that house, so I went about all that must be done until I heard the knock of day's break. When I said I must go to the master, she laughed and said indeed I must, for the master never waited for any thing in his life. I could not see her meaning so I left her there, seeming as though the night just passed had been naught but fever-tossed. Truly she is the strangest lass I ever saw, but strong as a beast in a field.

The master bade me sit and offered good ale and sweet white bread. In the morning light I saw a handsome man. Strong of face, with large nose and broad forehead. Ruddy-cheeked, but more through good meat than too much ale, I would think. And with good dark hair, thick and waving, all his own. Those eyes did hold me again and I thought his mouth cruel, though he spoke kind enough.

He asked after his lass and though I knew he had spoke to her in the night, I could not guess what she told him, so I bethought me to say truth, but only the smallest part.

I said she had not passed a restful night, but seemed over the worst and was minded to come down and sit with her mother this morning. I told him she was fine and young and I thought her very strong, so he need not fear for her too much. Then I promised to come to her every day if he wished it.

All the time I spoke he watched me close. Then he asked if the lass had spoke much, so I told him she had not, which was full truth.

He turned away and looked out of the window for a time, then asked which other folk I tended, so I told him I cured many round and about the town. But he would have their names, where they lived, their trades, their ailments.

I became angered by it. And his way of keeping his back to me when he spoke. I could not see why he would know what I did for any but his own and I told him so. Then I said though it might please Dundee folk to chatter like sparrows about their neighbours, I was Aberdeen and it did not please me.

He faced me with a stare then, and right angry he seemed. I saw how cruel he might be if any crossed him but I was affronted by him. Indeed, I was affronted by all in that house.

So I stood up, for I was sure he would tell me to go and I would not leave without taking my price from his wife. I was vexed at myself for letting anger speak before good sense, but could not see what else I might do.

He would keep on staring and twas then I saw watchfulness hid in those hard eyes. And questioning too. All on a sudden, I pictured again the way his lass looked at me, with old eyes in a child's face. And it came to me clear what secrets lay behind them.

I kept my face as still as I might but he saw my thoughts had reached a place he would not have them go. Then his eyes told me he feared discovery.

I know not how long we stood there, silent and staring as though each took the measure of the other's soul. I tried hard to think what his next words might be but his long silence affrighted me, and in the end I could bear it no longer. So I told him again, I never spoke of what I did for any I cured, but he could be sure I could send his lass to her marriage bed as perfect as the freshest new bud. Tis the oldest trick in the world, I think, and the lass might have contrived it herself easy. But I would keep her father tied to me by letting him think I need return often.

He saw clear through my bold front and all my riddling words, but I knew sudden he be a man well used to speaking riddles himself and putting fine front on rotting heart.

I never thought grand houses might hide such vile, unnatural things, though tis sure I have seen it before. There can be few curewives who have not. But only in the worst garrets, where ale-sodden folk lie huddled with too many bairns, like maggots on foul meat.

I see now there be naught but a scrap of silk between the highest and the lowest.

It seemed half a morning passed in that way but it must only have been moments before his manner changed. Twas like seeing the sun after a storm. He told me he was called Reid and asked if I had heard of him. I had not and I told him so. Then he talked of Pierson and Mudie, the Wedderburns, all the great men in the town, and asked if I had heard of them. I told him twas only suckling babes who did not know of them. Then he asked if I attended any such and I said I never had. I think the man cannot talk like other folk but must riddle all the time.

At last he asked my price and smiled right broad when I said his wife and the lass would have need of me for a while yet. So he told me I must attend them until they are both well, but come to him for my price each day.

All is so strange now. Tis as though I have crossed over a high wall from where I was before I lay in the Howff that long night, all covered in filth. I have put my mind to Reid's words and the strangeness of all in that house, but the tangle be yet too tight to unpick. James would have me tell him everything that passed but I am minded to give him only small truth, until I see where Reid's path lead.

Wee Annie and Wull came today and I was right glad to see them, for it seem there are few smiling faces about nowadays. Wull watched the big new guns brought into the town and when he heard Ramsay was put to finding cannoneers he sought him out. That Ramsay must be a kind man for he told him he never saw a braver lad, and he would fain take him when he had growed a mite. Twas not enough for young Wull, though. He goes to the muster at the Howff the morn's night to see if any company will take him.

Annie said she would never go willing to the Howff again and she would think our night there enough to keep Wull away too but he scoffed and said he feared naught and would fight for his town. Poor lad. Only ten years and already jumping to join the soldiering.

James told him Dundee needed more than gunners and

swordsmen and many of the bravest men in the town were rebuilding the defences. He said any man would be proud to join them and if Wull would go with him in the morning, he would find him a position. He will speak with Mylne, for they have been friends since they were lads and there is no mason nor carpenter in this town would not take on extra hands just now.

When the bairns had gone I said he had done a fine thing but he gave me a wink just.

He is a good man, my James.

Tis two months since first I stepped into the Reid kitchen and though I attend Mistress Reid often, today is the first time that cook spoke friendly to me. She went round and about it and said all manner of small thing before I saw what she wanted. It must be law in that house never to speak plain and simple. She said her lass was terrible poorly and naught she have done do cure her. She would have me go, but worried my price might be too high because I tend her mistress now.

I would get on the right side of that woman, for if she be powerful in the Reid kitchen, tis likely she will know her kind in other grand houses. So I told her I would not always take the shilling, for friendship come before putting silver in a pocket. She seemed well pleased and I will attend her lass tomorrow.

I cannot think how Dundee folk may be so slow-witted. Twas clear to me what ailed the woman so soon as I looked upon the wizened, yellow face of the infant lying beside her. But I must ask what I might do for her, if she felt pain and all such nonsense. There are some folk who do not like to hear truth spoke, even if their secret heart already hold it. They will tell only simple ailment in hopes small curing will banish great trouble.

So it was with her. She said her bones pained her badly and she had terrible sharp pain in her back but when I asked if there was aught else, she said naught. I saw no marks on her face, but she held her shift high up against her chin so tis likely the roses have crept up to her neck.

Tis truly a terrible thing. Men roam far and forget the swift pleasure they take in the roaming. But womenfolk pay the price always.

All newborn do carry briefly the light of ancient wisdom in their sightless eye. But hers held all the corruption and cares the world ever knew. Twas a poor shrivelled thing, its brow squeezed into an old man's hundred folds before a week's breath had yet been drawn. Its signal lay like a stone in my belly.

I could do no more than bring her simple stuff for the easing of her limbs and now I must think hard on what to tell that cook. I dread to say truth, for oft times the bearer of ill tidings must suffer punishment due to another.

Truly that pox be near as bad as the pest.

There was a man in Aberdeen that must go about always alone, for all feared to be afflicted if they speak to him and chance to take his breath at the reply. He wrapped half his face in a piece of linen, but I saw it slip down once when I was a girl and near screamed at the sight of that dead white skin, all wet and crumbling away at nose and ear.

Elspeth said he had been a sailor. She knew his sister, poor soul, that many folk shunned near as much. She said he went to an old woman at Cadiz port, that his shipmates swore could cure better than any other. She cut living fowl from neck to tail and had him wrap them round his member before the heart stopped pumping, so that as the dying flesh cooled it drew all poison from the living. Tis a cure for festering wounds too, when webs be scarce.

Mayhaps Spanish fowl are not so good as ours, or mayhaps he must join his ship before the cure was done. It matters not. She did not cure him and so he used the quicksilver ointments until he could no longer pay the pothecary. He died a shambling, palsied creature, cursing the day he was born from dripping, toothless mouth.

11

The troop is a disgrace. This town was safer when Major
Ramsay drilled ordinary Dundee men but he is gone and
Lyell do not seem to know how to keep his troop quiet. They
strut like cockerels about the place and fairly send folk wild with
their grand boasting talk. James says he would gladly lose a bit
of trade to keep them away from the alehouses. It seem they do
not come one or two together, like decent men, but in dozens.
Dundee men must stand in corners or be pushed to the floor.

He came in last night and said he would stand for it no
longer. There had been a fight because Miller the blacksmith
dinted the floor with a pair of them when they said he should
be thankful they guarded his town. He did no more than push
them over, but he be a great bull of a man with hands like
spades and so half a dozen of their fellows, too drunk I suppose
to have any sense left, set upon him. James says it did not last
long, for Miller be well-liked and none would stand by and see
him fight alone, but a complaint is to be put before the council
so soon as the guildry may see fit.

Marjorie MacAllister call me Mistress Butchart nowadays. She
was terrible afeared at first that I would tell folk of her lass, for
she is greatly shamed, though truly she could be no more innocent of blame. I told her I never speak of what ail folk, for I
would not wish another to do it to me. Then she said she owed
me more than she could pay.

Back and forth we went, Mistress Butchart and Mistress
MacAllister, in our little wordy dance of friendship until I said,

all round and about, that one such as she, in high position as cook, would surely know folk from all the great houses. She took my meaning clear. She gave no promise but I surmise twill not be long before I am called to attend folk who will pay more than a shilling for the simples. And she will take my dwale to her mistress each day I lie abed with the bairn, so I will not lose to the pothecary.

I am well content.

Mistress Reid be happy now. She told me Montrose is truly gone. Not killed, of course, but chased away. She heard tell he took his highland band into the south but Leslie's men had the better of them. It seem they took no prisoners. They even killed the women and bairns that had followed their men.

She care not that he still lives, though her own roof took fire and she might have burned in her bed. I would give much for that woman's good fortune. She hear at her own board, from folk who know, what I may learn only after it have passed through the luckenbooths and become a tattered, misheard thing in the journey.

I asked if any knew where he went but her talk do jump about like a flea on a collar and so I must listen to much nonsense before her eyes wandered to a picture of a stormy sea. Then she said, as though we had not spoke of him before, that Montrose was away abroad, to Norway or some such place.

She think there will surely be no more disturbance now. I was hard put to keep from laughing, or crying. What she would call disturbance have killed and maimed many good folk and left others with no shelter.

All able men are back at the ditching and stockading so the warring will cross Dundee again. I would give much indeed to know when that foul wind will blow so I must listen good and close to what Mistress Reid say now, so that I do not miss such serious words as may lie hid in her aimless chatter.

12

I have not thought to write here for so long but tonight I look upon my Alexander, who lie asleep like an angel and I would tell the women yet to come that he is the bonniest babe I ever saw. I have brought many into the world and I know there are few who do not look upon their own and see a beauty where others see only another bairn. But truly, I never beheld a finer-looking infant. He have thick hair and no blemish on him. Good long legs, he take them from me I think, and he be fat and strong. He do not cry overmuch, but tis a good lusty sound when he do. James see himself in the nose and brow but I see my father.

He will grow to be a fine man, my Alexander.

James have never stood so tall, nor smiled so broad before. I think his friends laugh a little at his boastful talk but tis in kindness and affection for him and the memories they hold of their own firstborn. I see him gaze upon the bairn sometimes with such a mazed look, as though he cannot believe the wondrous thing that lie before him. And once I caught him look at me in like fashion. I smiled to see it but only to my Alexander, for James would think I glanced upon a weakness in him.

Marjorie MacAllister did right by me at last for today she sent me across to a merchant house where the mistress was said to be taken to her bed in a fit of mad weeping and wailing and none could talk sense into her. Tis not near so fine as the Reid's but twould do well enough for half a dozen ordinary men and their families.

The woman slept when I went in to her so I waited until she woke, then must wait more while she wept again and gabbled she was ruined, that none would ever look kindly upon her now. And if she must hide from folk the rest of her life she would lie in her bed and eat naught, the better to entice death.

The more she gabbled the worse she wept until she could scarce catch a breath so I slapped her face twice, as hard as I could. She stopped then and stared at me, gulping like a fish new-landed. Then I told her who I was and that I must know what ailed her before I could do aught, staring close into those bleared eyes and talking the whiles of all the folk in this town who would be glad to have so much as one of her dinners to share among ten bairns.

After that, I set Alexander to face her, tickling him until he laughed, for there never was no happier noise. At last she smiled a little and said he was the bonniest bairn she had seen. When I saw she was calm I asked what had caused her to take to her bed. She huffed and sighed for a moment then said since I would hear it all over the town soon enough, she would tell me herself, for she would not have the tale sprout arms and legs as it went from mouth to mouth.

It seem her man is James Smyth, a merchant. His trade had suffered even before all the troubles came to this town, for two ships had gone down the year before and part of their cargo was his. There were others in like difficulties, Smyth had not borne the losses alone, but there was barely a shilling left in the house when the sea closed over the masts. So he must seek to borrow money in hopes that further trading would fill his kists once more. Twas not easy, she said, but in the end he met a fellow merchant, Thomas Watson, who told him he was now so hard pressed he could do naught on his own account, but he acted as agent for others. This Watson said he knew a man who would lend. I know of many such in this town. They are found everywhere I think. All quick to offer a pound or two to any fool, so long as he give four or five back.

But Smyth was keen. His wife said he would have run all the way to Edinburgh to speak to a willing lender. Watson said the man would speak only to him and so Smyth must await his reply. It took four days but when Watson returned, he had more than offer of money.

He said his man was sending three vessels to Danzig and Smyth could have what cargo space remained in them if he begin to pay back his borrowing the day the ships left harbour.

But if Smyth thought he could fill a fourth, the man would supply it and await payment until it returned to Dundee. In return, he must agree to bring back, hidden in amongst his own, whatever cargo the man had waiting at Danzig. Then he must store it until such time as Watson collected.

Smyth was not willing at first, for the man would also have him bear all the cost of the first ship to be lost if there were a storm. And then a share of the others if more perished. His wife heard many loud arguments late into the night and once or twice Watson left the house with angry words. But at the end of it, Smyth filled the ship. It made safe passage and though he paid dear when the vessel returned, he was able to leave his counting table in good spirits.

It might have been better for him if all four ships had foundered but the success of that first strange trade left him greedy for more, so he continued and prospered. Later, he joined with one or two others, the better to spread the burden of borrowing.

Watson would tell them which port held his man's goods and they would fill a ship or two with such cargo as folk in that place would buy. None could ever discover the name behind the lending, though they tried, for Watson would say naught but that his man did not wish his name put abroad. And that he was not one to be crossed.

But it seem Watson grew bold enough to cross him in the end. It seem he would not be content with such payment as he got for delivering messages and collecting his man's goods from Smyth's store. He stole some and tried to trade on his own account. And so he was undone, the fool. He had just sold a quarter weight of powder when the villain who bought it was taken by the bailies for trafficking with Royalists.

When Smyth's wife said those words my belly rolled. I had thought she spoke of no more than hiding a little trade from the excise man, a small thing to most folk with any sense. But supplying Royalists with the powder and ball they turned on us is wickedness beyond imagining.

The council fined Watson two hundred merks. Was it for the smuggling or did they seek to take from his purse enough to force him to name his man? Tis sure he named Smyth, for he is taken too, and I doubt not he will name his fellows. But if he also named the great spider whose web ensnared him, is there aught the council could do with it? Or will that spider stay hidden behind Smyth's name on his evil cargo?

Smyth's wife have not heard what is to become of him. She know nothing of his fellows. She never thought to question her man so long as he provided all comfort. I cannot think what to make of it. Smyth is either the biggest fool that ever lived or a villain fit to be hung.

I have writ the tale short here but she took an age to tell it, always shifting about and sighing as though she suffered pain unbearable. I have spoke to women in this town that Montrose left new widows and none have carried on so.

I was fairly sickened.

In all that long listening I bethought what I would do when she asked me my price. If I took a shilling, I might betoken myself as wicked as Watson and her man. For where would she get it if not from his purse?

She said she was a poor innocent, punished for the folly of her man but mayhaps he only did wrong in trying to do right by her. If I had no thought in my head but the newest foreign manner of fashioning silk into a gown, and went amoaning and awailing to my James that I must have more, no matter how hard pressed, might he not go willing into wicked foolishness too?

I cannot say. I am not that witless woman and my James is not ensnared in another's web. Tis all too tangled for me tonight and I will set it aside until sleep have sharpened my wits.

If twere not for my bonny Alexander I think my days would be drear indeed. There are few nowadays who do not frown where once they jested. All are tired of this war that seem to have no end. The ditch at the west is finished and another begun to the east. I watched them hammer pales about the East Port to mark the line until they reached Lownie's house. It sit outwith the Murray Gait, with a fine yard at the back, but twill not be there much longer, for naught may get in the way of the ditching.

James says there are some returned to the town from army service who have not been paid. Tis a disgrace. What manner of man would send another to risk death then keep his proper wages from him? Tis not even as though any might choose to stay at their work. When the drum roll, none may deny it. But if no man at all be paid for soldiering, mayhaps one day no man at all will follow the drum. Mayhaps the generals might do the soldiering themselves, make a tourney of the thing, and let folk wager a shilling or two.

What foolishness I write today, but tis indeed a happy fancy that my Alexander might grow old in peace, knowing sword and gun only from his father's storifying.

Reid was in fine friendly manner today. He offered wine, tickled the bairn and talked of all manner of small thing. I could see he wanted more of me than to pass pleasant time but I like such small chattering in his room. So I smiled and gave pleasant words back until he showed his true intent. He was afeared for Mistress Smyth, he said, for he had heard she was poorly and that I tended her. He would know what was amiss so that he might come to her aid, now the poor soul was left alone.

I was surprised, for I did not know I had been seen at the

Smyth house. I told him again that I speak naught of the
ailments I heal. But he just waved a hand and turned to the
window, as he like to do sometimes. He said he cared not for
her ailments and if I thought as much I was less wise than he
had gave me credit for. He thought only of the material circum-
stance of a poor woman. Long words that took me a moment
to swallow.

He would know only of her condition, as he was pleased to
call it, without her man. When she expected him home. What
food was ate in that house. Whether the fires be lit or no.

I thought then he had dallied with her. That he would know
how long her man would be away, the better to apportion time
to her. I did not like it much, but with earnest entreaty all writ
upon his face, and his promise that none could give him such
intelligence as Grissel, I was minded to think it mattered not
to me what such folk did with their time.

And I thought since nowadays every bairn in the street be
gabbling of Smyth and Watson, there surely could be no secret
left to keep.

So I gave him the tale and from the set of his head I knew
he smiled within himself, though I know not why.

The minister said those two are cast out into the wilderness, ever
more to wander in darkness. When I told Reid he asked if I
believed everything the minister said. I did not know how well
to answer, for all must hold what a minister say as truth absolute,
though they speak only such words as the General Assembly
instruct. Some things they thought good not long ago they call
wicked today and make laws to stop them. In my secret heart I
think the only truth I know is what my women have spoke one
to another since the beginning of our line, but I would not say
aught of that to Reid. I would not even say it to James.

Sometimes Reid's words sound simple enough but they can
set my thoughts trailing like ribbons behind them and tis the
hardest work I know to follow each and stop it tangling with
another.

So I said only that I believed the minister's words would serve me well if I but walked with head bowed where they might lead. It seemed to please him for he laughed aloud and said, 'We will speak again, I think, Mistress Butchart, of ministers and suchlike folk.' Then he smiled broader than I have seen him do before.

His eyes were full of laughter but I knew he did not mock me. I thought he looked at me admiring, as the winner of a close-fought hand might look upon the man whose cards near took the pot. I cannot make the man out but I do not fear him now. Tis my belief we are alike and naught but great friendship lie behind his smooth and fine-stitched coat. When I left that room I felt I walked taller. Twas a great pleasure to me, though I think I will not speak of it to James just yet.

I have done little for a three-week but nurse my poor Alexander. He made another tooth, but with far more pain and fever than the first three gave. Now I think a fifth follow too soon, for his cheek be still too red and his fist never away from his mouth. He will sip a little warmed hegbeg ale, and it make him sleep better, but the pain be sharp enough to wake him often. The poor lamb be tired beyond sleep now.

Last night James came back from Jaks all a-babble and today tis spoke everywhere in the town. Folk say tis sure the fighting will stop now the King have given himself up to our army. None know what will be done with him but they think tis enough he be taken. That he will do Scotland's bidding now and we will have peace.

I know little of the ways of kings but I would think they do no man's bidding but their own.

I went up the Law to see what my mannikins might show. I took care to pin holly into a fold in my shawl, to keep my Alexander safe. The mannikins were begun by my hand but when I left them there they gained their own life and I would not risk my bairn's peace if they looked ill upon my visit. I passed some soldiers but they did not remark me. Naught seem so harmless as a woman with a bairn shawled about her.

I found only one remaining. It face northwards so I know now whence Montrose will come again. I walked far out then, towards the Sidlaws. Twas foolishness, for if he had come today I might have walked full into him. But I had in mind naught more than to see if I might find trace of the rover folk and speak with the woman who saw war in Dundee.

I saw no one.

13

I am hard pressed sometimes to find the makings of a decent dinner. It seem no matter how much malt he turn, James cannot bring home as much as he was used to do. Tis all the fault of that Stirling who sniff about for his excise like a terrier after rats. There is no hiding from the man. When Bailie Davidson came back from Edinburgh, he told the guildry they must pay excise for a year only. That was two year ago and now the council fair love the taste of the tax gathering. I jested of it with Mister Reid, though I had not thought to do it. He is truly a clever man for he set the why of it before me quick and simple.

The Estaits in Edinburgh have changed the excise law. Before, the council must send all they collect to pay for the army. Then if aught was left, some would be returned. I never heard a dafter thing in my life, for only a fool would expect money back.

There be a new law now, though, that give the council leave to keep back from the tax gathering all the cost of quartering the troop, giving cloth for soldiers' coats and such like. They must send only what remain to Edinburgh. Tis even dafter than the first, but it keep the money in our councilmen's hands until they be pleased to let some of it go. I see now why they be in such a boiling hurry to collect it from the likes of James.

Mister Reid would know how I looked upon the King's surrender and I was well pleased to think he would hear my thoughts on such great matters. We spoke longer than ever before and though my words were a mite hobbled at first, from the strangeness of it all, he listened so close I soon grew bold enough to speak as I might to James. And he did not contradict me at every turn, as my man is so pleased to do. I think he took my words serious because I have thought them all oft times before. So when they were said aloud they ran out well formed and did not jig about like sparrows all a-bicker in the mud.

We spoke of Montrose and I said we had not seen the last of him. And that when he came back twould be from the north. I was not looking directly at Mister Reid as I said it but I turned just at the finish and caught him staring at me with brows upraised. He settled his face again in the blink of an eye, for he is not a man who like to show his thoughts there, but I know I caused him great surprise.

He asked how I might know that. What I heard as I went about the town. If I knew of any who trafficked with Royalists.

He spoke so fast, and looked at me so strange, it grew worrisome. So I told him any fool could see the council awaited his return too. Why else put all our men to the ditching and the wall. Or knock down all the houses outside their lines.

He turned away to his window, as he always do when he ponder. When he looked upon me again he was smiling. He jested I was so uncommon farseeing I must take care to speak my mind only to him, lest others mistake me for a sorcerer. I laughed along with him, though tis dangerous folly to make light of such things.

Then he grew serious again and said I saw aright. Montrose had indeed tried to come back, and from the north, but had been halted. I asked what stopped him and must hold my breath for a moment, sore afeared he knew of what I had done and wondering what to say when he faced me with it. But he said only twas the pest that gripped Meigle now. No soldier could conquer such a foe. I nodded and made small words in agreement, all the while seeing naught but my mannikin staring out across the Sidlaws and feeling great fear and pride together.

I kept this town from harm but tis only right that fear should sit upon me too, for great knowledge carry great power on its back, and so must be kept away from those who might use it ill. Mister Reid said something of the sort. He have uncommon wisdom for a man. He said knowledge and power, though they be great things, are built from many small things. Our women have always known this. Each have added a small new knowledge and wisdom to the old she was given. And now I carry all their power.

He spoke of how safe Dundee might be if only there were some, or even one, with foreknowledge of an enemy's thinking. I said twas true indeed but I could not see that any would run to a bailie and say they scryed a danger that would befall Dundee next Lady Day. He said I could make a serious remark sound uncommon amusing, but that scrying was a game for daft old women and foreknowledge was often no more than sharp-witted surmise born from many small scraps. A word or two overheard, or a glance between seeming strangers. Boxes in a warehouse that only saw bales before. All these things might mean naught in themselves, but to sharp wits they might add together to form a signal clear as a beacon.

He rang a bell then and when his man came, asked for wine and said we would have cold beef, and ham on a platter too. I had only a thin rabbit to put in James's broth that night and took swift thought to refuse, but then I thought of all the nights he had come back from Jaks full of ale and pies and tall tales, so I ate and drank with pleasure.

When we were done, he asked if I was minded to keep the town as safe as he wished it and of course I said I was. Who would not? He knew my worth as curewife now, he said. Mistress Reid was better than he had seen in years and his lass, praise be, so rosy on her wedding day. I know that well enough, for I watched her leave St Mary's and there never was such seeming innocence as shone from behind her lace. Her mother said she is mistress of a fine house in Forfar now.

He said twas clear I was uncommon sharpwitted and he could think of none he could trust more to seek out all the little scraps of knowledge we had spoke of earlier. Armed with those, he could set the great men of this land to keeping the likes of my

Alexander sleeping sound and safe. I told him naught but simple truth when I said I would be glad to do whatever I might to assist, but knew not where best to begin.

Then he told me he would send me to other grand houses when their folk wanted curing. I must take no more than fair price from them but must listen close to all that was said and bring it to him after. He would have me become so oft seen that none remarked me. He spoke very serious and told me twas the most important business he had ever done. He prayed I would be willing but he knew that if I did what he asked, I might have no time left to cure others. He would not see my purse shrink, he said, so he would pay me for every scrap I brought him, according to its worth, but never less than a shilling.

I said I must think on all we had said but would give him answer as soon as ever I could. He smiled and said I did right. Then he took my hand and bowed low over it.

I never knew a man with finer manners than Mister Reid.

Now I must look upon it all from every compass point and try to picture a balance, with all I may gain in one dish and all I may lose in t'other.

Tis a year today since my Alexander was born and I know not where the time have gone. It seem much is changed but tis no more than the shortlived change snow bring. The land beneath is the same and all that folk fear most rides yet upon it. I still carried him when first the pest looked upon the town. It chose not to come then. Stayed away so long we dared hope it might never step across the Sidlaws. But then John Fithie's bairns were took, poor blue-spotted innocents, and him sent away to the Sickmen's Yeards.

James says his grandfather, the first burgess in the Butchart line, saw Wishart preach to the sick of the Yeards. He came here when the pest raged through the town and there was not a soul who did not lie awake at night fearing and praying to be spared its deadly touch. But Wishart did not fear. He thought only to bring comfort to the afflicted, and the pest did not touch him. James said his grandfather wept aloud when he was burnt. There was none in Dundee did not curse the evil that set such a man to die upon sticks and tar barrels as though he were sorcerer, not one of God's own. And folk cheered when word came from St Andrews that Beaton was killed to avenge him.

The Cow Gait Port is called Wishart's to honour him. James says twas built not long before he was born and its stones will stand as proud memorial so long as Dundee live.

Fithie's bairns were just the first. So many have followed there is another lodge built and a watch at every port in the town. Folk say they get six shillings a day, so there will be no shortage of men willing to mark all who would try to cross their path. Bailie Dickson of Rotten Row was at Edinburgh before and he have brought their ways here. Nowadays, when the sick are sent to the lodges, every single thing in their house must be took out and washed at the meadows, or if it be cloth it must be burnt. Bailie Dickson writes what is took and if folk live through the trial and are let into the town again, they get back what may be left. Now I think tis hard enough for folk to sit the four-week in the lodges and then be scrubbed head to toe before getting leave to go home, without taking away all they possess too.

Wee Annie came to see me, bringing her brother Tam with her, who is ages with my Alexander but only half the size, poor soul. I doubt not his mother be too hungry herself to feed him aright. If I put out bannocks with our ale, Annie eat only part and hide the rest when she think I do not look. She be ever smiling, though, and we had a grand time playing with the two babes. Later, I took her with me seeking berries for she says she have never done it before. Tis sad she do not know what good things may be had for the taking, even within town walls. I gave her some small gowns I made for Alexander in the spring. I had been minded to make two into one bigger but I could not bear the sight of her poor ragged brother.

I asked after young Wull and she said she is soft on him. As if I could not see that for myself. She be right proud because Mylne took him when he went to see Duncan the piermaster. Wull rowed them out to have a look at the west pier and listened close when they spoke of the cost of timber and wages and suchlike. He told her he listen all he can for tis the only way he may grow to be a man like Mister Mylne. Tis sure the lad is clever and I was minded to hear for myself all he could tell me, so I had her bring him for his dinner the next day.

It seem Mylne do not always find work for him and Wull seek where he may for more. He would away to sea if he could but his mother is widowed and he must stay by.

We spoke of the pier work and he said the piermaster have been reporting damage to the council long since, but they pay no heed. The thing be rotten, and it creak and move about in the tide so much there is no sailor nor harbourman who do not complain to him every day, though he can do naught but ask again and again for the money to mend it. Mylne said half the folk in the town press the council for money in these times and the price of timber would make a man weep. Tis so hard to get nowadays folk might believe there was no trees left in the world.

Wull would have gone off with James when he went back to his maltings but I held him back, saying he must take some meat for his mother. When James had gone I made much work out of preparing a crock for her but talking all the while, light-voiced, as though what I said was of no more account than the price of a loaf.

I spoke of how grand it would be if there were any man in Dundee who could make short what the council took long to do, if they did it at all. If such a man only knew what was said between the likes of Mylne and the piermaster, and was minded to act when the council did naught but talk, then Wull and others like him might have work aplenty before long and the harbourmen might dance all together on the pier, though the ministers would surely set their dourest frowns and call it wickedness. He laughed at that and I knew he liked the thought, for he said twould need to be a rare strong pier to take the weight of Mister Duncan a-dancing with Mister Mylne.

Now that lad will look always beneath or behind what he see and hear, so I took the talk away along small paths for a time, but always coming back to getting a penny here and a shilling there until his mind had filled his pockets. Then I stepped back right nimble to the main road and said I took my curing work to some grand folk nowadays. Mayhaps if good, hardworking men like Mister Mylne and Mister Duncan could speak as free to them as I do, there would be less hardship in this town. But that was not the way of things, I said, for hardworking men spoke free only to each other or to hardworking lads.

I watched Wull put his mind all around it and hardly breathed as I waited to see how he would jump. But then Annie did the thing for me. She said if I took all that irked the likes of Mister Mylne to important folk in the town, naught but good would come of it. The lad dithered about a bit for show, for he knew we both waited to hear what he thought, and so I told him I would see if aught came of what he had said already and he must bring Annie back in a day or two. Then I gave him the crock for his mother and sent the pair of them off.

Reid be right pleased, though he believe he hid it from me. I think he want all I may get from the harbour and I will take another shilling or two from him before Wull's tale be all told.

Bailie Mudie cried today that the Lord's name be profaned by the Saturday market so it must be moved to Fridays. Will Provost Kinneiris have his wife repent this Sunday for all the years she profaned when she believed she did naught but buy eggs and beef for her man? Tis pure foolishness and folk are tired of the ministers picking away at all they knew as good in the past. They will call a wedding feast profanation next, though it seem some are already poor dull shadows of what we had when I wed. Jonet McKenzie bring me scraps from the Pierson house and seemingly his lass would have no wine nor whisky at her wedding, only the plainest fare and no dancing nor jesting at all. But she married a minister, which is as well, for she go about always with downcast eye and praying look about her. She be too prayerful for my belief and secret sly I think.

Jonet says a body could wander a month in that house and never cross the same room twice. Tis nearly as grand as Scrymgeour's castle, but more fanciful. I never saw a house set upon stone legs before, and in a haar it seem to me like a ship afloat.

I have spoke to James of moving to a better house, for I would have two rooms and a yard if I could. I do not like to live so hard up against my neighbours when the pest be all about. I know of one at the corner of Seress Wynd that look on to Over Gait and is higher off the street, so we would be further away from the muck. Tis dearer, of course, but I get so much out of my scraps nowadays I could near pay the price myself, not that I would ever tell James. He do not like me to speak too often of Mister Reid.

But mayhaps tis not wise to spend more just now when James may be called to the army. He says twould be madness to send a man of his age away to England, but there be naught but madness now. This town, that was all Covenant, and flayed for it, be now pleased to stand Engager. It truly pass my understanding how such a thing could be. The King is Scotland-born but know his land not at all.

And did he not cause all the warring from the first with his English prayers and anointments at the crowning and suchlike Popishness, that his own folk would not put up with?

Mister Reid told me the why of it. Tis a rare tale indeed and if I could follow the twisting and turning of all the players in the game I might find a thread of sense in it.

He said we fought on the side of the English parliament because the General Assembly saw that they are plain folk, with no more taste for silk-slippered bishops than us. But we could not afford to send a great army, so they made agreement to pay us and we went to fight for them.

When we won, the King surrendered to our army because he feared what the English would do to him and he knew they would not let him sit upon his throne again. We kept him safe and said he might stay King if he only sign the Covenant and put Knox's plain words into every church in England. But he would not do this, even though we had protected him from his enemies.

And all the while the King was refusing us, we waited for the money the English had promised. But it never came. There was much angry talk, and letters going betwixt one side and t'other until at the end of it, they said we would get not one penny unless we handed the King over to them.

So we gave him back, for he would do naught we wished of him. And the English got rid of him as well, to an island off the south coast, far away from London.

But still they did not pay, though they had everything they wanted and our men had fought and died for them. Such wicked, conniving liars could never be trusted again. So now it seem we would sooner have Charles back on the throne than treat further with the English parliament. And we will fight to put him there.

I told Mister Reid I could not see why we wanted Charles at all, for we have gone on well enough without him all this time. His foreign ways do not suit us and our kirks do not suit him. We fought before on promise of payment from one side. Are we to believe t'other will pay us this time, or will the council begin to take excise on each breath we draw?

He said my wits were as sharp as ever, but I must take care never to say aloud what else might be taxed for fear an exciseman lurked near and took it to the council. He is a wise man for jesting my anger into the air. Anger be a foolish waste unless it change bad to good. Tis useless to try to unravel the plotting and trickery of kings and councils and parliaments. Ordinary folk can never know what whispered villainy and connivance do pass between such men. They do only what bring them greatest wealth and pleasure.

They care not how many die, so long as the dead were not of their kind.

They care not which side they stand, but jump from East to West and back again, contriving a new name for themselves each time and thinking ordinary folk so dull-witted they will forget the old.

And they tell themselves their twists and turns are the deeds of honourable men.

After, I spoke with Marjorie MacAllister. One of her sons is braboner and he be called among the dozen their guild are to send, though he have five bairns and another to come at year's end. His wife is fretted half out of her wits thinking upon how she will manage if his soldier's pay be late. Marjorie dare not even think on the worser fortunes that might lie before them. James says the maltmen are called to send thirty, more than any other in the guildry, though they know not why it should be so, nor yet how the Dean of Guild will decide who must go and who may stay.

I know none with the stomach for it but there is talk that some will take the place of a man called if enough coin pass between them. I will find such a one if James is put on the roll. It cannot be long now before he hear.

Half the town was at the shore today, shouting and cheering to put the men in good heart and praying they all come home safe. The inns were full last night, with the fortunate pouring so much ale into the unfortunate tis a good thing twill be some days before they must aim a gun. I had not known James would take so strong against paying another to go in his place. When I spoke of it, he said twas naught but lowest sly cowardice to seek out a hungry man and tempt him to bear another's burden. He said Death would not be tricked and would find each man at the hour appointed, whether he be on a battlefield or safe in his own bed. I gave him sharp words in return but even as

I said them, I felt proud to have a man so fine upstanding. He was not called and we are blessed, my bonny Alexander and me. I pray twill not be long before the inns are full again.

Oft times I think on that house at Seress Wynd and wish I had just took it and faced James's anger down after. Now we have the pest hard by, I spend my days bothering the bairn, seeking out a cheek too flushed, or his nose running overmuch. Tis in the next close. And from Aberdeen, too. Andro Nicol, that is so well liked, took in a lodger who was lately come from there to be footman. The lad died so sudden Andro must call in the physicians. They found marks of the plague, so Andro and all his folk are to the lodges for the four week. Now there is word that one of his lads is dead too so the inspectors are about all the houses here daily. I am so afeared for all of us. What would become of my bairn if James and me were took? Who would care for him as I do? I would give much to have Elspeth alive and sitting before me now. There never was such a press of sadness and fear on my back before.

14

There be great trouble coming. The sense of it thicken the air.

King Charles beheaded at Whitehall gate in England by that traitorous parliament and army on Tuesday 30th January 1649. Prince Charles proclaimed King of Great Britain, France and Ireland at Edinburgh Cross.

Lyon, King of Arms.

I have writ the words just as they were gave today at the Mercat Cross.

There was a silence at first. Folk tried to tell themselves they had not heard aright, I think. Then a muttering began and ran back and forth among the crowd. Not loud, but terrible with anger. Since Argyll seized the Edinburgh parliament, every town in the country must be unbending Covenanter, no matter how many favour a kingdom over the new common wealth. Dundee be no different.

But killing a king. Tis a vileness that cannot be supported.

I went to tell James so soon as I could and he could hardly believe it. Tis the strangest thing to hear folk talk of naught else at all, or see two at a distance and know from hand clutching cheek or mouth all sudden that one have just told t'other.

I even saw some weep as though they had lost a father. Mister Reid said they wept for the loss of something all had thought unchangeable. Where there had been a crown was now darkness and folk feared it greatly for none have seen its like before. And who could foresee what king-killers might not do to lesser men?

He spoke truth. The fear be terrible because tis not a fear of known things, that may be spoke about and soothed by wisdom and kindness. There be no wisdom to tell what best to do when a king is dead, not in battle or sickbed, but in treachery.

Mister Reid said the Prince be abroad but will come back now Scotland have declared for him. Tis sure he will bring Armageddon in his wake for this kingly game do not end, like Mister Reid's, with black or white cast down and a handshake between two players. The first Charles was not killed only to leave way for the second to sit upon his throne.

I have not seen the kirk so full for half a year. James would go to hear if the minister had any more word of what was to be done now. I went too, but the man had no new words to add to the Lord Lyon's few, though of course that did not stop him prating so long I near froze. I would sooner trust to my own wisdom nowadays than listen to their dour and dreary rumblings of damnation for us all. If the pest will take good and wicked alike, and kings may be murdered as easy as vagabonds, what purpose to kneel and pray for deliverance from evil? There is none.

I have been thinking on Netta McFarlane's words. James says I should have known that flitting to Seress Wynd would cause talk, for he told me time and again we were fine where we were. He seem to think I have forgot how oft he said those words. That man was so hard to shift I thought we must stay forever in Sea Gait. But in the end he agreed twas not right Alexander should grow up in one room when his father grew up in two.

I have not put on airs and I cannot think who might tell Netta I do not see my old neighbours nowadays. She would give no name, of course, saying she could not remember rightly now and I was to pay her no heed.

I asked Margaret Ramsay, that I see near as often as before, and she said Netta had naught but clouds in her head. A happier soul there never was, but none took her words serious for they tumbled out too many to count and faster than a body could rightly listen to.

Margaret made me laugh for tis true indeed. Netta's tongue have a life of its own and I feel for her poor man. He be the silentest creature in all Dundee.

But tis easy enough to say Netta be a harmless fool. I still cure a fair number of her West Port neighbours and if once her words do settle there and cause a doubting in even one, I may lose them all. I must go careful I think. Mayhaps twould be as well to set a watch on the woman. I will see young Annie Fraser tomorrow.

Mister Reid made me a gift of sclate and chalk not long ago and I have been showing Alexander how to form his letters. He can write his name now. Not straight nor neat yet, but each letter clear, and him just four years and a half. James says he will be advocate before his beard see light of day, though there would have to be a miracle before we could pay for it.

I can scarce hold a pen but it must be writ. Montrose was here and folk cheered for him. Cheered and hailed him as great soldier. He came from the north. Not proud-mounted as before, but bounced hard side to side in a rude cart. Bound hand and foot like a criminal, but alive and hale. Some said twas a disgrace he was left so ragged.

The fools in this town must give him a bed for the night, of course, as though he had not burned enough from theirs, and when he was seen again in the morning he wore new garb. He goes for trial to Edinburgh.

I hope they hang him and I hope tis done slow, in front of a spitting mob.

James says I set my thoughts too close to Montrose. That we must think on better things now. When he talk like that I can believe the malt have befuddled his wits past mending. If Montrose was beat in battle and engaged for the prince we must call king now, what manner of fighting do we await?

Mister Reid says the prince must sign the Covenant before he wear Scotland's crown, but the English Ironsides want their bishops and no king at all. Young Wull heard that name from a sailor that was lately at Newcastle. Tis a name that bring with it pictures of great armoury and might.

I have had no stomach to put aught here for two weeks or more but today I set the finest dinner James have seen in a twelvemonth, with claret too. He looked at me strange, but I said naught at all of what lay behind the feasting. Tis enough I know the beast was quartered and his head stuck upon a pike at Edinburgh Tolbooth. I heard it said today. Perth have an arm and Aberdeen too. The legs be at Glasgow and Stirling. Tis a pity Dundee got naught, for I would have relished watching a shrivelling limb be picked to clean bone by uncaring crows.

He is not a grand figure of a man, the new King. Too small and near girlish in all his beribboning and velvets. A foreigner by dress and manner.

Wee Dougie McFarlane shouted up that Alexander must come quick if he would see the grandest thing a man might see. That bairn do make me laugh for he be but six years, and small with it, yet he always cry himself a man. Alexander near fell out of the window trying to see what was ado then ran off like a hare before I could catch him.

There were folk hurrying along Over Gait so I followed and saw him and his men by St Mary's. He looked to right and left. Smiled and waved. There was much cheering. Many hands reached out to touch the hem of his cloak for luck and good health. Tis very droll that folk who so lately spat upon the notion that a king's power was God-sent could return so quick and thoughtless to ways older than the Bruce.

Alexander came back well pleased but dirtier than ever I saw before. His breeks, that are new-made, were all stiff-streaked with bird muck and moss. It seem there were more than a dozen lads climbed up with him to the roof of the meal mercat when the horses stopped at Will Spens Close. I shouted long at him that no king be worth a broken neck but he paid me no heed, for James was laughing at the caper and saying twas a poor sort of lad could not climb like a fly where he might.

They tried to follow the King's party in, but a soldier was set at the mouth of the close, so they climbed back on to the roof again to see if they might see aught through the windows of Lyon's Room. Twice up there, indeed. Tis beyond my imagining why lads get such wild foolishness in their heads. And my James be no more use at the chastising than a buffoon. So now Alexander think he made fine sport today in pleasing his father and fretting his mother half to death. He look like an angel when he sleep, the sweet lamb.

When I told Mister Reid he laughed as much as James and said my lad was set to do great and fearless things. He be no different to any ordinary fool sometimes. I think men see lads and remember their own happy daftness so fond they forget that oft times one small slip may lead to crippling or worse. Mary McIver's bairn, that was so bright and hale, do no more now than sit empty-headed and a-drool since he fell under Murray's horse.

Mister Reid would know all who come and go to the Spens Close just now. Tis not easy, for I have none there and must depend upon Ella Hamilton, who run the doxy-house by Yeaman Shore. There is always a watch, but all soldiers will pass the time of day with a bonny lass and Ella's be younger and cleaner than most. She keep them tight-bound to her too, so once she have told them how to set their nets, their seeming idle chatter draw as much from the guard as he know.

There are great men come there this last few weeks. Committees, they style themselves. A fine long word for a gaggle. Ministers of the kirk, fine-suited wigheads from the law chambers of Perth and the Edinburgh Estaits. Mister Reid would press for names but I cannot get them, for the soldiery be told no more than to let them pass.

Tis hard to please him just now. He be like a man driven. He would know all that come in to the Pack House, where it be from, where it be shipped to. I think he would know what every carter carry in and out of all the ports of the town if he could. I cannot fathom it.

Marjorie MacAllister said strangers be in and out of the house all the time now, even at night, and not for wine nor cards neither. Men she have never seen before run in all covered in two or three days' road dust and stay barely long enough to swallow a pot of ale before they are away again. Mistress Reid frets once more and she had been fine and smiling so long since. She says she feel harm pressing all about her, as if a storm would burst soon. Tis sure there is a different air in the house. I feel it myself but tis everywhere the same and I have no time to fret. Mister Reid press me too hard these days.

Young Wull have sharp eyes and ears and since the harbour-master took him on he have brought me much. There be more ships coming in from home ports than abroad now and the cargo stays in the town. The men at the shore say tis all from rich folk in Edinburgh and the big lairds in the south. Wull have heard some say they will not be long in following their treasures and they will make Dundee the richest, grandest town in Scotland. He think there will be work for all in building great houses and provisioning fancy tastes. He think the great Edinburgh merchants will put so much sail in and out of Dundee the shoremen might double their number and still run all day and all night.

He can picture grand things ahead because he do not yet know how trouble tomorrow may be signalled by seeming good today. I would not take his pleasure away, but I am too old for such innocent hoping. The war never stop. Our men are away to England again, under different banner, but still called to bleed and die as before.

Shiploads of rich men's treasure coming up from the south signal naught more to me than a scramble to hide from plundering soldiery. Dundee will be the richest prize any army ever gained and when they come they will not leave until they pocket the last groat.

I ran about so much for Mister Reid lately I hardly had a minute for my own and now he is gone without so much as one word beforehand. I have half a dozen or more to pay for their scraps and naught from him to pay it with. Twill have to come from my own purse. I must write all here so that I may reckon well with him when he return.

Wull Greig	For name of eighteen ship @ 3d	4s 6d
	And for forty name on boxes and trunks various into Pack House from Monday past to close of Saturday following @ 1d	3s 4d
Ella Hamilton	For Flora's counting : Twelve ministers @ 1½d	1s 6d
	For Marie's following : Five likely advocates, out West Port and on to Perth Road, all with heavy satchels @ 2½d	1s ½d
	For Teeny that saw Scrymgeour, Wedderburn and Mudie go in and stay long @ 1s	1s
	For Ella's good will @ 5s	5s
Davina, Letty, Maggie, Irene	For visitors to their masters' houses @ 2d	8d
Jessie	For word of a letter from	

Mudie to Guthrie @ 3d

		3d
	17s	3½d
Then half again	8s	6d
		1¾d
	£1 5s	11¼d

Ella cost me too much but there is no help for it. Tis not right Mister Reid should leave so sudden without paying me. If he were here I would ask Two Pound and get £1 7s 6d easy, but now I must await his returning before getting aught at all. It anger me so, for I never had to reckon on long waiting before. I must think long and careful on how much over the Two Pound I should go.

Mistress Reid be away too and that have never happened before. The house be half stripped of its finery. Marjorie says there was never such a rush to wrap and pack away, and a cart came late last night for boxes and trunks of clothes. She is terrible afeared.

I told her I thought great trouble be coming, and worse than Montrose. I did not say it to frighten her the more, I had thought any fool in that house could see it. But she looked long and strange at me. Then she asked how I might know what lie ahead.

Tis clear as day to me and it pass my understanding why she do not see it. Mister Reid be a rich man who seem to know more than most. So I surmise that if he leave with all his chattels, tis because Dundee is not safe.

I began to tell her something of it but she would not hear me aright. All the servants were told he must away to Denmark on business and his wife would go with him, for she had took a fancy to the notion of seeing a foreign land.

Marjorie would hear naught else but that Mister Reid be away on business, as oft times he is.

Thrice over she said it but her eyes spoke different words. So I told her to pay no heed to my surmising and rattled on to small and happy things for a time, to settle her. I got her to draw us some ale and gossiped long and light, but hiding hints in amongst it all that she should seek safety.

It took an age but at the end I knew she had flattered herself twas her own wit brought me down to the cellar. I was fair speechless at the size. Tis fine and dry, and spread under the whole house. Room enough for all the Reid servants and the Butcharts and a dozen more besides. I will go careful these next weeks until she believe she cannot be safe unless Grissel sit down there with her.

Annie and Wull are to wed in three weeks. They came tonight to tell us, so pleased with themselves they were a gladness to us. She asked James to give her away and he be fair delighted. He will buy Wull a new coat. The poor lad was half froze last winter and his sleeves stop half up to the elbocks now. I am to go with Annie tomorrow to buy her cloth for a gown and we will make it here, for her mother have no table. Twill be such a pleasure to me, for she is turned into the bonniest lass. I will lend her my wedding cap, that I have treasured careful.

They had not sought giftings from us but we would do no less, for they are grown like kin. James asked what manner of revelry they would have after, but they seemed shy to talk of it. Doubtless they have not so much as a spare sixpence, so he will speak with Wull tomorrow. He is minded to clear a space at the maltings and set tables and benches, for there will be a fair few attending. With brothers in the bakery trade, and them knowing folk in all the others, James will make a grand spread at little cost.

Tis a pity there can be no dancing. Those ranting fools in the Assembly say that merry weddings be fruitful seminaries of all lasciviousness and debauchery. Tis just as well the ministers repeat those words near every week else none would know what they mean, nor how to swallow them without choking.

We might manage a reel or two if the bailies did not go a-hunting sinners so terrible keen, but those men could hear a fiddler scrape a jig in Perth. So we must just whistle soft and jig lightfooted.

15

Alexander have took well to his letters but James will not send him to the school yet, though many begin at five. He think the lad should not be worked like a man in a freezing schoolroom when he may get letters from me and numbers from him. It seem godliness and good manners make the rest of the lessons and he get the first at the kirk and the second at home.

I cannot say I think him wrong, though I would see my lad set fine like Mister Reid one day if I could. He was at St Andrews and said there be no finer place to exercise sharp wits, though it be fearsome breezy and cold even in the summer.

I miss talking with Mister Reid. I would give much to hear what he think of all the ordnance and a whole regiment of horse sent out of the town today. There was two special carts additional, loaded up with poles and bales of heaviest linen. David Elder said twas all the parts of a contrivance called pavilion. Seemingly tis like a house that may be carried about the country. The poles are stuck into the ground and then the linens draped across and tied. Doubtless His Gracious Majesty will think fondly on Dundee when he sit in the warm and dry watching our men eat their porridge under the stars. David heard it said twas all gifting for the King, to show Dundee reverences the day of his birth. He believe that tale as much as he believe he will live a hundredyear, but he can keep his face straight and solemn like the rest of us when he must.

*   *   *

I found Marjorie hiding away today, for fear twas one of the
bailies calling her to help Reverend Guthrie. I have pushed
barrowloads of turfing to build up the walls again, like all but
the oldest crones and the babes. There was even a birth and the
lad will be christened Gilbert, to honour the minister, for he
be a kindly, well-loved man and the women are willing to do
his bidding. So are the bairns. My Alexander and all his friends
have cut and blistered hands from running all day helping
their mothers. But good Mistress MacAllister have done naught
yet. I am right angered with her but did not say it. She hold
the key to my hideyhole and I will have it from her yet, though
she have turned stupid as a mule and must be treated with
cunning according.

More strangers come in every day, rich and poor it matters
not. All carry the same tale. Edinburgh is took, and Stirling,
and now Perth too. I know not if there was much fighting and
burning, or if those places surrendered to keep the peace. Now
Dundee harbour fortunes from all of them. More booty than
any army ever saw, I think. Will we surrender quick and hope
to keep the peace, or will our garrison resist long and hope to
hold tight to the treasures? The town is crowded. The owners
of all the gold and such will want to resist.

I know as though I could see it writ here that Montrose was
naught but a pinprick to this town. English ships are sighted
off the Tay bar. Wull ran in to tell me. And there was word
from a Fife coaler that thousands of horse and foot move up
from St Andrews. Dundee stands alone for the King. We are
dead if we do not surrender.

I think Marjorie MacAllister have lost her wits. Tis sure she
have aged ten years in as many weeks. She do naught now but
sit at the kitchen table, twisting her hands in her apron.

I spent half a day trying to get her to open the cellar again
until I found the stick to beat her with. There be but one maid
left in the house, a lass with no kin. The rest are away and by

the look of Mistress Reid's room they did not go empty-handed. So I sent the lass out to draw water then told Marjorie what Mister Reid would say when he returned.

I used what words I thought he might, walked up and down as he do and set my brows to louring as his can. To tell truth, I near believed I was Reid myself, so well did I wear his boots. At last she spoke, all mewling and halting, of how wickedness in others should not be laid at her door. She had served the Reids so faithful. On and on she girned, like a cringing cur but I got her moving at last, bringing down what bedding remain, and went in to the cellar for another look.

The door opens into the kitchen and fit very tight against the wood t'other side, so twill not be easy to break through. The cellar be divided into six parts, five open and one gated and locked for the wine. There be a full sack of meal and another of flour. And I saw two hams and a whole English cheese, three barrels of beer and I know not how many pound of candle.

When the lass returned she asked me what was ado and I was in weary readiness to spend half the night re-telling the tale. But she listened close to every word and when I had done, asked only how many folk would be sitting in the cellar when the trouble fell upon us. I was so surprised at finding a sensible head left in that house I must sit down and catch my breath while I counted. A dozen of mine, for I will bring Margaret Ramsay and hers if I can, and Annie and Wull. That will fill two spaces and leave three for what folk Marjorie and the lass might fetch. Grace, for that is her name, just smiled and nodded her head then settled Marjorie to making a great pot of porridge, saying it would keep well and she would get as much bread and bannocks ready as she might before the fire must be put out. Then she told me to make all ready for myself and come back in the morning if Dundee passed a peaceful night. If not, she would let me in on thrice three soft knocks.

That lass have wits, though well hid, and I am happier than I can say for the knowledge of it.

16

I have cursed them for days but they do not stop. I had not thought it would be so bad. I had fancied the army that could beat a Leslie would be well-drilled, but it seem there is not one that is not so maddened with drink and blood-lust his ears be stopped to the shouts of his commander.

There be gaps between the stones at the top of the wall, level with the street, and we take in turns to keek through the holes when the screaming stops, seeking sign that this bloodstorm may end. But even after six days and nights there is none.

The woman lie there yet but bleeding no longer, thank God. Eight soldiers set upon her, threw her down and took her one after t'other. I think she knew naught by the time the last two had their turn for she had stopped screaming. She might have been dead when it ended so still did she lie, but then she stirred and the last to defile her gave a shout of such rage when he cut her head off it near killed me to stay silent. I think he even stopped the breath of the other vermin in his pack for a moment, for her blood sprayed high and wide. Covered them head to foot. I had hard job jumping down before it covered my eye at the hole.

I knew her not but she must never be forgot. Tis why I have writ her here. If I lay where she is now, who would write for me?

It grow harder to keep all silent in this cellar. The bairns are terrible afeared when they hear the screaming. Grace brought a bundle of old scrim down and it have been near the usefullest thing we have. When the noise come close we stuff our mouths with it to keep silent.

Only yesterday, or mayhaps twas the day before, I cannot tell time now, she spied soldiers at the front door. They hacked away for an age before they broke it open. We looked up at the boards as they ran about the rooms above. There are some gaps between, but not many, and we showed no light but until the footsteps left, we hardly dared breathe. After, I prayed in thanks as I have never done before.

Tis quiet outside just now, though the noise of pain and death continue not far along. It smell like half the town burns. If this house be fired we must run. But we are safe for another night, I think. Stone and sclate do not burn easy.

I brought my book for safe-keeping and now I write in it for soothing. I would go mad, I think, without it. The roaring of the fires puts me in mind of stormy seas. When I was a lass I liked watching the wild-tossed waves, though I knew such water could kill unlucky sailors. I have pictured the water easy enough but can bring no memory of its clean smell into this foul air. I will walk to Broughty with James and Alexander when this trial be over.

James roared and huffed when first I said we were to sit the war out in Reid's cellar. Oh, he was angered that I could find a place better than he to protect our bonny bairn. But his roaring was naught but wounded pride and I healed that easier than first I thought. He is a fine man, my James.

There be so much wickedness outside these stinking walls I can scarce believe folk inside could make it worse, but they do. Marjorie's sister have been caught dipping into the last of the meal. We must eat raw meal and flour now. Naught else be left. James says we have been down here twelve days. All agreed we must share equal but the longer we stay the smaller the share. All are sick. All hungry. But all agreed the bairns must come first. That woman steal from bairns and her own kin. A curse on her.

*   *   *

Tis dark now. The streets be quieter and the holes are blocked again to keep the candlelight from showing and stop the draughts. I can almost fancy I sit at my own hearth. I am glad beyond words to be alive this night and James and Alexander sleeping peaceful.

I had thought we were discovered but they grew tired of trying. I saw my poor man weep silent tears of fright when we heard them hammer at the cellar door. They had been running about the house again. We listened to the footsteps, the faint laughter and swearing, then I went to watch for them coming out. But they did not.

At first there was thick silence, then came thumping, scratching and banging. They are worse than pigs. They broke their swords against the metal. James took the handle off before he locked us down here. A swift last thought and right clever it was for we could hear them poking this and that into the lock. We prayed it would not yield or if it did, that the smooth metal would resist scrabbling fingers.

Oh, those men were crazed with rage that one door should be locked against them. The man who built this house knew not how many would bless his skill, for that door moved not an inch under the battering. At the end of it we had no strength to move to spy them leaving but after long, long silence, we knew the house was empty again.

I had a sense of change at first light and all must have shared it for they woke together and lively. I think we be like animals now, that do not speak but know by the smallest twitch of a tail that one hear a sound all must heed.

Fires still cracked far off but there was a stillness in the street, naught moving but the flies, thick-swarming over the dead. Then we heard far-off shouting, not wild screaming but drill commands. Not long after, the first soldiery came with carts and began piling them with corpses. I heard one puke as he picked up the poor soul they killed outside our cellar. We had stuffed the holes well so I could not see him, but I listened close. I heard him cry that he could not touch the head. He will see her every day and night until he die, if justice live here still.

James was all for running out to see if his maltings yet stood and he was not best pleased when I shook his arm hard to quieten him, in front of all the others. But in the end he saw the sense of waiting as I counselled so we sat silent again, taking turns at spying through the holes, until we saw ordinary folk about the street.

Some crept along like shades, fearful and haggard. Others ran back and forth, calling out for their kin. Whether seeking answering call or mourning the dead, I could not tell. Most took a quick look down upon the dead they passed, unwilling and sick with dread, then moved on. I saw one wave the flies from a face then scream aloud in grief. Another moved swift and toe-tipping like a rat, head turning side to side in sly ever-watchfulness, then bent to pull a ring off. But all went un-molested by the soldiery that passed them.

The sun was high when at last we came out and it near blinded us, so we retreated into the kitchen until we could see easy again. It took no time at all but served well as excuse, for on a sudden, it seemed none wanted to leave the shelter of the house. I feared to see wider than the patch in front of it, to join the other folk in the street. I did not want to see what had stolen their souls.

James went out first. Alexander ran to him and would not come back to me when his father told him. I watched them go, James striding and the lad running to keep up, hands held tight. I had thought I would run to see if our house still stood but my feet would do no more than drag as slow as a snail. The town looked like the hand of God had torn it asunder in rage.

Our house be half gone so we will stay here until we have four walls and a roof again. If the Reids return before I am ready to leave, they must carry us out kicking. We have made our place in the garret and they have room enough to spare. It took two days before I could venture back into that cellar, and another three to get it scrubbed out as clean and fresh as when we went in. Margaret Ramsay helped me willing. There is just a hole in the ground where her house was so she came back, but stayed no more than a week. She will not be beholden to a stranger, she said, nor taken to the bailies for sitting at a rich man's table. As if there was aught upon the table.

Her man is gone in the fighting, though she do not know where he lie now. Mayhaps tis with the other poor unknowns at the foot of St Mary's tower. Just so many bits of limb and flesh torn too small to say how many, or who they were. There be funerals all day still. Some have took months to die of their wounds. Some are dead of the cold, for folk sleep in the open still. There are barrikits everywhere, and little huts and shelters made from all the burned and broken wood and stone that fill the streets. They keep the rain out, but not January cold.

Alexander killed three crows today and they stewed fine with hegbeg. Crows make tough eating, but chewing long make the belly think it hold more than it do. I sucked on a wing and ate most of the leaves. James and Alexander do not like them and they need their meat more than me.

Tis easier to get meal now. At first the soldiery set the millwheels grinding and folk were hungry enough to take what they doled, though I know none who smiled or looked them in the eye, and many who did like me and spat upon the ground as they left. But now there is a Dundee miller again, though prices be more than folk can bear.

James be angered that I write here. He says when all is lost what good to scratch endlessly as I do. Alexander hate it when we shout and run off. But each must do what he need to make a terrible time easier to bear and I would do this over all else. Tis made for my women. Twas begun in happiness and innocence, to tell of good things and leave the lessons of our lives.

Now I see the lesson of my life be only that evil may begin

small and unheeded, like the first few drops of summer rain. But it can turn in an eye's blink into a flood that destroy all in its path. It sees not the good nor the bad. Tis blind to babes and cripples, to the lazy and the lover of toil. It treat thieves like princes and turn honest men into thieves. It turn other women's sons into murderers. It might even do the same to mine when he grow old enough to be mustered, though I pray he have seen enough now to know the difference between soldiering and slaughter.

And this evil come not from fallen angels or any such kirk-maister's nonsense, but from ordinary men, given power out of the ordinary, that let them kill their fellows with less thought than a terrier give to killing a rat.

I curse them all. I curse the King that fled. He caused death beyond reckoning and now he sit abroad again. I wonder if he have his pavilion still, that David Elder made. The man should rot for sending poor David to the Howff.

I curse Monck, sitting in his tower now, right in the middle of the town, watching the funerals pass. None know how many died. Hundreds, a thousand or more. And half the living might as well be dead, so silent and empty-eyed are they. He killed a whole town, yet still he stay. Tis sure he like peace and quiet for he have made silence here.

I have not laughed so much for an age. I saw Young Wull and Annie today. They hailed me at the Cross and said they had broke into an empty hut at Sickmen's Yeards and sat out the two-week there. I could not find them to bring to the Reid cellar and thought they were lost. And in their turn, they thought me dead, seeing my house all burnt and broke. Wull said the English stole sixty ship out of the harbour. They could not carry the booty they took from Dundee in less. But they are lost. All lost. They got no further than the Tay bar before they foundered. I could not stop laughing at the thought of it. The thieving vermin got naught at all and half were drownded in trying.

*   *   *

The General seem fearsome keen on making proclamation. Twas read out today that if we report any violence against us by his soldiery he will punish the offenders according. I wonder what more could be done against us.

His punishing be a rare entertainment, though. There was two soldiers given thirty stripes and set in the Tolbooth on bread and water not long ago for highway robbery. And another two that got the wooden horse.

Tis a grand thing that horse. The men are set upon its sharp-ridged back with hands tied behind them and muskets to weight their ankles. They fairly scream even before it be pushed along. I laughed to see it, though James could not abide to watch. He called me unnatural, and I laughed again until he stamped off in a fury.

He proclaim what folk we may see. We must report any stranger that come into the town. If we do not, we are to be fined right heavy. Now how may I know that a face that is strange to me be not kin or friend to another? That proclaimance be naught but a terrible temptation to liars and gossips, or neighbours with a grudgement. Who would bother to report unless they be paid for it?

He proclaim against fornicators and drunkards, as though whipping and ducking in the river would stop them, any more than a day in the stocks ever did before. James would not mind a few more drunkards about the town, though he would see Dundee men at the ale pots, not soldiery. The maltmen had hopes of more trade after the council fixed the price but at 2s the pint folk scarcely buy, and there is little gain at that price.

I fare better now than for a long time past, for there have been so many births of late. I cannot take much from the mothers, but halfpennies and pennies grow into shillings slow but sure. Most have little, and some poor souls naught but what they get from such kin as are left to them. I have done a dozen or more whose fathers are dead. Tam Nicoll and Leckie Hill would have had a son apiece, and fine lusty infants too. James put five shillings in the maltmen's kist for their relicts last year.

Some poor lassies will never know which English soldier forced them to childbed. I have great sadness for them. Folk like to forget a bad thing, but a bairn bring it to mind every time its mother set eyes upon it. Grizel Mitchell, who live near the Lady Well, says she have delivered ten such. I had not known her before, for she is lately come from Forfar. Her man is carpenter. There are many such folk coming in to the town for work now. I do not think Grizel be over-blessed with brains but tis sure she know some curing, for I have seen her about, picking the herbs and leaves. I must see she keep to her side of the town.

There was a messenger came up from the harbour today looking for Marjorie. Just a lad, younger than Wull. He said he brought orders for Mistress MacAllister but she grew confused when he spoke to her. Nowadays, she be but a thin shadow, no more master of the Reid kitchen than a blade of grass be master of the air that blow it.

It seem Reid will return in a three-week and would have the house ready. James have put much into patching the front door and mending broken chairs and such, but I think the Reids will find a poor place notwithstanding. We have no roof to our own house yet, so we will not be out of here. Tis no matter. The Reids think a cook awaits them and they had a fondness for me, both of them. So I will cook. Mayhaps we will get fat on it too.

I never thought to hear such words, and after all the work we put in, too. Mister Reid was not best pleased to have naught but half empty house to come home to. After I fed them, rabbit stew and fresh bannocks that was looked down upon as though the makings had not took me days to find, they walked all about the house, remarking on blackened walls and lost bedding. But I took care to say all he had missed since the first day of September last. I left nothing out. Not one fly-blown corpse.

After, I stared long and hard at the man then summoned the breezy voice I was used to use and told him twould not be long before he had his house back as fine as it had been before, but he could see well he would never get his cook back. So Grissel must do for now, since Dundee was left so empty of folk, each man do two jobs and each woman the same, caring for bairns with t'other hand besides. He smiled small then, very small. But he took heed and so I sent James and the bairn off to make up his bed and set a tankard of good ale before him. There is much work to do here now and I will have it all until our house be fit to live in again.

I went to the Murray Gait port today with six hard eggs to put in Jeannie's hand. Some of the hammermen met at the Howff to resolve what might be done to help and it seem they garnered £3 between them. They be right angered that Tam Philip was treated so, but Colonel Corbett be a vicious piece of work. Hated here above all others of his kind, and his regiment the same. They look upon us as though we were gutter-dirt.

Tam did no more than say to a friend twas a disgrace Governor Lumsden's skull was still spiked up the steeple. That none could disrespect the dead like the English. But one of Corbett's men heard him and pulled him up hard. Shouted that he should mind his mouth and learn to be grateful to English men for bringing order to his filthy barbarian town.

He shouted at the wrong man. Tam stood near alone at the end of the fighting, lost two brothers, his father and his uncle, more friends than he care to count, and an eye besides. That soldier was lucky Tam did no more than shout back, call him no worse than scourged hangman, thief and loon.

But Colonel Corbett and his men do not like it when barbarians speak their mind. It remind them of what they did.

They gave Tam twenty-one stripes of the lash at the Mercat Cross today and banished him. Jeannie and the bairns must go too. Folk watched the whipping without a sound but they stared at the soldiery with so much hatred the silence screamed with it. Then they crowded up to the port and made quiet goodbyes, hands slipping bannocks, pennies, halfpennies, even a jar of ale into the handcart to say fare ye well.

Reid told me today that a town all burnt and broke be not a cause for bewailing but a chance to build a better in its place. I was talking of how tired folk are of hardship and misery. How folk who had buried too many dead, and lost all they owned, could not even put food enough in their mouths because trade be so bad. He would make light of it. He said there were hardships in each life but none lasted forever. I must set my eye to looking forward, not back.

He smiled as he spoke, testing how long I would hold my tongue. I know his games well now, and play them much better than he think. So I smiled back, though I boiled with rage, and gave him the word that the council are to nominate burgess quartermasters, now that we are overrun with so much soldiery the magistrates cannot do the job quick enough. I said I might try to learn who is to be put to the Over Gait. I knew before I spoke tis James and his brother, with one of the Yeamans, but Reid will not be told that, only the consideration for keeping his house to himself.

I cannot think how I was so innocent before. I once thought him a fine, high-thinking man. Now I know he want only to sit at the heart of all trade in this town. If he gain report of other men's business he may buy a cargo here, send another there before they do, and leave them waiting long for more trade. Or he make sure they must buy from one of his agents.

I care not. Each must look out for himself nowadays. Reid got our house repaired far ahead of all the others in the Row and I am right glad to be home. If I can only find another few well-placed lassies, I may settle with him in a month or less.

17

James came home with a horn for Alexander today. Auld Duncan can still carve bone better than any sighted man. The bairn be fair delighted with it and ran off, wooden sword in hand, to muster his friends. They cannot get enough of playing soldiers. It put me in mind of Grizel, that was mother to Helen.

Her father carried a sword, though he died peaceful in his own bed. He went abroad to fight the English. Left a year to the day after she was born and did not return for ten year. When he came back, even her mother must stare long before she saw her man beneath the foreigner's green and red garb. He brought home a tale, terrible and true, that folk have spoke of ever since.

The English wanted a foreign throne and were fighting and besieging in a land not their own, as they like to do. The foreigners could not make enough of an army themselves, so they brought men from Scotland to fight on their side. Some of these men, Grizel's father amongst them, were led by a girl. She was the greatest commander any ever saw, though she was so young and fair. The English laid siege to her town and for eight days she did not rest, spurring on the townsfolk and her army to fight ever harder, ever harder until at last they saw off their attackers.

Then she led their prince to be crowned. But her country was divided and though the folk in the north wanted the King, some folk in the south did not. So the fighting went on until the girl was captured by the southerners and they sold her to the English.

When word went about that she was took, many followed. They had in mind to watch close and find their chance to free her. But the chance never came. The English and the southerners knew that thousands had followed her willing into battle. They saw she was loved so well she would always be a danger to them. So they accused her of treason, heresy and sorcery.

Grizel's father said she prayed when they tied her to the stake, and the crowd prayed with her, their voices growing louder as the flames began to roar across the faggots and tar barrels. After they killed her, the Scots turned for home. They saw no man could win against a people who would abuse the law so.

Grizel was one who would know as much as she could about all this world hold. Twas her father put that hankering into her. His wanderings abroad had gave him a questing nature. She told Helen that if she had not learned the wisdom, she would fain have been a man. She wanted to go abroad and see how foreigners live. She wanted to have her father's way of hearing what the King said to all his people, then sitting down to pick away at every word and find the real desire of the man.

Her King was the first James, the one who promised there would be no place in his realm where the key did not keep the castle and the bracken-bush the cow. Grizel said that meant the man would have all Scots protected under the law. He wanted everyone, rich and poor, to know his intent and he had his proclaimings read out at mercat crosses and kirks across the land. It seem like little nowadays, but I write of a time when poor folk mostly went about never knowing what manner of master they served, beyond the one who took their tithing.

Alexander was fair surprised when I told him I knew of that king and many more besides. Nowadays, he think he know more than me or his father ever will. We laugh, but sometimes he bring home learning beyond ours. The dominie be a fine man, if a mite too fond of talking about his days at the university. He tell the bairns often that if they work hard and pray hard, mayhaps some will find themselves in St Andrews too. The man is a dreamer. Most of them wish only to find themselves in front of a hot dinner every day.

But he weave lessons of olden times into his dreaming talk and that please me. We got fair fired up with the tale of the first James for Alexander gave it well. Indeed, he could not be stopped. He strode up and down the room, waving his precious sword as he spoke of a lad sent across the sea for safety but kidnapped by English pirates and put in prison in a tower in London. Twas eighteen long years before he could claim his throne.

The dominie said he was a fine king. Poet and music-maker besides. But he had too many enemies and barely a dozen years later he was murdered and even his own kin had a hand in it. Tis ever the way with kings.

Alexander got a rhyme about it.

> Sir Robert Graham
> That slew our King,
> God give him shame.

Seemingly the killers got tortured three days before they died. Tis a grand thing, the rhyming and I like it well.

Alexander was red in the face at the end of the tale and James said he wished a dominie had gave him stirring tales when he was at the school. But all he got was the tawse for writing, 'The fear of the Lord is the beginning of wisdom' with small L.

I was right shamed today at knowing how soft my life is. I was away out beyond Hill Town picking the herb and I saw the rovers. I was so glad to find them again, I ran up, smiling. But they stood back from me, as though I threatened. It took much talk before I learned that Morgain be dead of hunger. I could not speak at first. Twas as though she shook my heart from beyond and berated me.

All of Dundee have known long that hunger lie upon the land again and though all bemoaned the cost of it, most left an extra penny or two at the kirk for the feeding of the vagabonds that are everywhere amongst us now. But vagabonds ever roam about a-begging, and we have felt so poor ourselves these last years. I had never thought the rovers could suffer killing-hunger, for they are better than cottar folk and grassmen at the trapping and they know what wild roots and such may be eaten.

But my friend is starved dead and I knew naught of it until today. Her kin told me they are shunned always, but worse when fat townsmen must feed vagabonds. They told me half the country be dead or dying. My poor, wise friend. Her death have put a paining tightness in me.

Wull says the first gale of winter will finish the harbour yet still naught get done about it. The council have been asked times without number for money to make repairs but it seem they have none. Now that is truly a wondrous thing. They squeeze all the excise they can get from the burgesses then make it vanish. Do the shoremaster see it go? Or do he go down to the river, lifeblood of this town, and watch it eat away at the rotten piers while the council turn our silver into air, and he make promise again to rebuild. There be no sense to it but sure as day follow night, when the harbour be lost to wind and water, the council will squeeze even harder to replace the excise they lose from all whose trade centre upon it.

Grizel Mitchell become more of a botherment to me. I see her at every turn. I was talking of the portsmen with Margaret Ramsay for her brother be carter there and seemingly all complain worser each day that the shifting pierings slow their work. Margaret looked past me as we spoke and at first I thought twas because we stood in the way of folk passing by. But then she did it once more and I saw a frown start so I turned and there was Mistress Mitchell, eyes wide with the effort of listening. The sight of that woman fair got my temper up so I sent her scuttling off with sharp words in her ear.

Alexander have so much of his father about him and the likeness grow more every day, though folk say he favour me. I cannot see it, aside from the red hair. He be but thirteen years, yet think himself a man now that he be half a head taller than me. He will not settle to the maltings, will not attend to what I tell him and would battle with James all the time, and over naught at all, if I did not put a stop to it. Tonight I watched him wear his father's way of stamping up and down the room in search of his hat before he marched off hotblooded and shouting over his shoulder at James. They be like two stags, old and young, that bellow and lock horns until old give in or die. I do not know where the time have gone. It seem like no more than a year or two since he sat listening to tales of fairy folk, or crying while I dressed a skinned knee.

Poor James be too old for it all, though he stamp about still, waving his arms and roaring away about all the ungratefulness and disobedience in the world wrapped up in one fool lad. He wanted to pass his maltings on, have his only son's name writ in the great lockit book of burgesses. But he must give in now and let the lad away. For scratchit breeks and a head full of spindrift there be no cure but the sea. When he go, I know not which of us will feel the weight of silence more.

18

I cannot recall the like of that storm. Twas as though all the demons of hell flew over the town tearing off sclate and thatching as they went. When I went down to the shore this morning I found half the town there, gazing all disbelieving at the flotsam that was the piers. I had known twould be bad, from the stink coming off the meadowlands north of the town, but I have never known such a wildness before. There was half a dozen ships anchored that could not get up to Perth in time. They were battered, two mainmasts broke that I could see, but afloat and all souls safe. The councilmen stood in frowning group, muttering and shaking their heads. Too late. Perth will have the trade now and Dundee the poorer for it.

The houses did not fare much better. Half the roofs be gone and folk at the top soaked to the skin all night. Grizel Mitchell came to see me, all drookit. She be an irksome creature, but I felt right sorry for her so I set a pint of hot honeyed ale to her hands and sat her before my fire to dry. We spoke of the storm and what she had lost to the rain pouring through her roof. She do not hide her woes behind a smile and a jest but I listened long, for I thought that now she be widowed, hardship may press heavier on her back. Twas how we were when one of Ella Hamilton's girls came in.

She was quick enough at the sight of Grizel to say she would not keep me, had come up just to see all was well with me and mine and such like nonsense. But she was dressed for her work and looked uncommon fancy in broad day. I could see Grizel's eyes widen at the sight, so I hurried the lass out the door and followed half way down the stair until I could take her whispers unseen. I was back and sitting before the fire again in an eye's blink, but I could see from the way she kept her face all carenot that Mistress Mitchell would not be shifted until she had sucked all the meat off that bone.

I would gladly have seen the back of the woman, for I wanted to get to Reid quick, but she gabbled on until I thought I must scream. Then, without me seeing it coming, she asked what I was about at the shore the night before the storm. She said I was seen throwing leaves and twigs into the water. And some folk said I made spells.

All I did was throw holly leaf and roddin berry in to keep my lad's ship safe. Mayhaps I threw old words in behind to strengthen their power against evil. If I did, I have no memory now, but the old words come to me at time of great worriment sometimes. They are naught but harmless salve for troubling thought and I was too took up with thoughts of my lad to heed any who stood near enough to hear.

She fairly drooled with the joy of telling me no fearsomer storm ever came to Dundee before and word be abroad that the Devil's stink came off the boiling river. I let the fool sot have her say. I even drew her another pot of ale, the better to bring out all that hid behind that reddened, smirking face. If I have enemies, and now it seem I do, I must learn right quick the paths their plotting follow or I may stumble all unknowing into their trapments and webs of jealousy.

And she is an enemy, I think, though I saw her as too stupid to warrant the word before. She want me out of her way. She would take my curing from me, but she must think again. I will let none hamper me. But I must think hard on how to stop her mischief, for loose tongues be dangerous when they lick seeming righteous ears.

Reid laughed aloud when I told him Ella's lass had been called to the great manse to deliver scourging and bring forth sincere repentance. If he knew the price his secrets fetched, I doubt not the good minister would indeed repent sincerely, but

tis none of my affair. I gave him the Mitchell woman's tale of
the storm being summoned, though I did not say twas me at
the heart of it. I tried to discover from him if he had heard the
same himself. He did but roll his eyes and say he thought I had
more sense than to listen to the maunderings of witless old
crones. Then he brought the talk back to what he want me to
bring him. I must cast a wider net than ever before. The man
would know all that is ado in every corner of this town and
half the country round about.

He told me the Lord Protector of the Common Wealth is
gone. Dead on the very day he broke Leslie at Doune Hill, eight
year since. Tis an omen. Mayhaps the stormwinds heralded his
passing and broke our pierings to signal that death had loosed
his iron grip upon our land. It seem he named his son to follow
on. Reid said some English call him Tumbledown Dick.
Whether the man be a sot or mere gangle-foot he know not,
but tis sure there is great change to come. Monck remain the
whiles, but Reid have the right of it when he speak of change,
for the sense of it crack and glitter the air at the edges of my
knowing.

All be a wonderment to Alexander now and we fairly love to
hear him speak the strange tongues he hear abroad. He bring
us gifts. Strange fruits, and herbs too that foreigners use in the
pot, not for the curing. Tis because he is young, hale and ever-
hungry that his eye seek out cooks not curewives.

I doubt not it seek out foreign maids too, but he would not
speak of that with me. I fret myself oft times that he will set
his heart upon a foreigner and settle abroad. I might never even
see her. I might never know the next woman of our line. Tis
truly a worriment.

James chaffed when I spoke of it. He said Alexander be not
near full-grown to a man, yet he have enough grown man's
sense not to entangle with wives and bairns yet, foreign or no.
But when the time be right, he will have sense enough to settle
in Dundee, that hold his own folk and all a man could want

besides. When he finished, he rubbed my cheeks with both hands, as he was used to do long ago and bestowed a kiss full on the mouth. It raised a hot flame of love I had thought long smouldered to naught but soft affection.

I have asked Reid for paper. Tis such a price now, but he buy great bundles at a time. I told him if I had it, I might copy letters borrowed from here and there. I had to use my own yesterday. Jessie, that is maid to the shipwright, brought me a letter her master had left lying on his table when he went to his work. Twas naught but lines of names and numbering that brought no picture to my mind, and I do not even know if Reid will want it, but I gave a shilling. Twas for Jessie's daring, and for the bright mischief she shared with me. I know not why I liked that running and hiding so. Mayhaps tis old age gifting me a last foolish spring before my legs can run no more. But I have not rejoiced so much in devilment since Elspeth sat me on her knee. Twas grand.

Tis the strangest thing. Monck's troop were so hated after the blood storm there was none in Dundee who did not turn away when one passed, for fear his eye would behold the murderer of kin. Then folk grew so they did not see them, even when their eye happened upon them. Tis as though near ten year of soldiery passing to and fro every day rubbed the sharpness off memory and left it sitting quiet, like sea-polished pebbles. And like pebbles on a shore, most folk did not remark them, though more than a few picked up the bonnier ones to wed.

And now it have ended. Sometimes folk will look twice at a place where a soldier was used to stand and wonder what be amiss. I have done it myself. I am right glad to see them gone but they have left an emptiness that seem new to us.

19

I stood with all at the Mercat Cross to hear it proclaimed. Charles sit crowned with gold in London town. When I think on all the trouble that followed upon his crowning at Perth, I could near feel pity for English folk. The Provost spoke long. He sat all silken and agleam on a black, deep-muscled steed. I could scarce hear half of what he said above the cheering crowd. And half the rest was words that must be chewed over a year or more to get their meaning.

After the proclaiming, he led all the important men around the town. Walking the bounds they called it. Tis an old tradition the Provost said might have lain lost and forgot if he had not gone seeking in Wedderburn's great library to find fitting tribute for a king so well beloved.

There were volleys from cannon and musket, and fires were lit upon Corbie and Tenters. The whole town was out drinking and laughing and dancing in their light. Full in the eye of ministers that had called dancing the Devil's work not a week before. Some were seen to lour and rail against it but folk paid no heed, for the wine and ale flowed as fast as the river.

I thought of our second Helen today when I watched a poor nag die trying to pull a cart full of stone from the town wall. When the harnessing came off twas difficult to see it had gone, so badly galled was the hide.

She was mother to Grizel and rare prized for her skill with horses. They whispered in her ear all that ailed them, so she could cure them better than any other. Twas a horse with a badly galled back that spoke to her of the cowbane. Folk thought she was mad when she went picking it, for the smell alone may render a body falling-down giddy, and many a beast have died through eating it. But this horse told her it might be boiled and used for poulticing so she tried, and within the week the galls were healed.

I have not writ our women for too long, so I will put Helen's mother here now, who was Effie. She was named for Euphemia, who was wife to the king folk cried Old Blearie. Twas Effie taught Annie McBride what our women's anger may do.

Annie's bairn was cut in the leg and festering. Effie had made offer to cure the cut long before, but the woman would not pay her price. So the bairn got fevered from the wound and wandered away one night, when his folk slept and the snow fell thick. In the morning, when he was missed, his mother ran all about, screaming and crying that the bairn had been took by the fairies and all such nonsense that women will say when one of their own be lost.

Effie searched with all the rest, and stayed long after even his mother thought him took by wolves. And she found him. Near dead of the snow sleep but with heart beating, so she took off her shawl and wrapped it tight about him. She breathed warm life into his death-searching mouth then ran back to her own hearth. She warmed him, cleaned his black sores and bound them thick with webs. Then she carried him home to his mother.

The woman swore she would do anything to show how glad she was her boy was home. So Effie took off her cap, held it out to her and asked that she fill it with meal. But Annie McBride started up weeping and wailing and said she was a poor woman with naught to spare and Effie must wait until winter was past. Effie did as she was bid, but when she went back, Annie McBride said again she was but a poor soul with naught to spare.

Now Effie knew she had three fine sheep in the outfield so when she must leave empty-handed again, she went to seek out the wilfire. She picked two bundles. One for the finding of the boy and one for the healing of the sores.

Then she pounded one bundle and pressed the paste into limpet shells. T'other she mixed with what bere she had left and when dark fell, took all out to those sheep. She got hold of the biggest and fed it the wilfire mash to inflame its liver. And while it ate, she pressed the shells close against its hide, to bring up the blistering, then she covered all with the long, thick wool on its back.

It did not take long. When the beast died Annie McBride ran about weeping and wailing again and saying to all she stopped that Effie had killed it. But Effie had strewed the ragweed that fairies ride from the carcass to Annie McBride's house. And when that was seen, folk said twas the fairies took the sheep, to teach her to pay what she owed.

But they never were close friendly to Effie again. They feared her and gave her wide distance. No harm ever befell her after, but folk marked her for a witch and she learned to live apart and say naught of herself to any but her own kin. Tis from her our women got the taste for keeping the knowledge to ourselves.

Reid showed me a rare thing today that he got from Edinburgh. Tis sheets of thin paper and on them is writ what have happened lately. Reid says tis named for a Roman god that was messenger to others in ancient times. Roman or no, tis writ in plain words and I got a look at a tale about Montrose. It seem Edinburgh gentry dug under the gibbet and lifted what remain of the man, and another they call Hay of Dalgety. They paraded the pair of coffins through the town to the church at Holy Roodhouse. His arms and legs are to be brought to join the rest of him. God help us all when that carcass be whole again. Mayhaps that Thomas Sydserf know naught of what Montrose did here. He write long and admiring of the trumpeting and cannon-fire, and the cheering of Edinburgh folk as the coffin passed, velvet draped as though it carried a king.

*   *   *

Grizel Mitchell will be sorry she crossed me. She was bold at first. Said if folk would use her over me, twas their affair. So I told her twould take me no more than a week to bring all of her women over to me, for I am known in Dundee as skilled healer and she be no more than a dirty, careless old sot. She fairly screeched then, saying she would not be spoke to in such manner. That I am known in Dundee right enough, but tis for giving myself airs and thinking myself better than I am.

Stupid nonsense, all of it and she crumbled soon enough when I stared her into silence. Then I frightened her more when I said I would have her in the Tolbooth for regrate. That shut her reeking mouth tight for the councilmen cannot abide such garret trade. I could see fear skirl across her face as she turned my words over in her dullard head and thought on how to play the game now. She chose the sorrowful face and twisting hands of a penitent. Said she knew I was in the right, but she be poor widow-woman now and only did what she must to earn the price of a loaf. There was no harm done in selling the odd cup of meal to others like her. What a sly-mouth she is.

I left her well warned to keep away from my folk and it seem she paid close heed, for she is away to Forfar, and just as well.

Tis so drear with Alexander away. His ship came in just before old Yool and he stayed for the New Year, but I know not when we will see him next. He said he wanted to sail distanter seas now and would sign on the first East Indiaman he could when he got back to Bordeaux port. James tried his best to seem glad, but I know he fear for his lad. Tis said the storms be terrible in those eastern waters, and we will not know how he fares from one year to the next. I wish he would settle here. I cannot think why he seek always for new sights to see. But we sent him off with smiles. I got the best piece of beef I could find, and James brought in wine and whisky. We thought if we must say faretheewell for years, it should be done with a finer dinner than he will eat for years.

I got him to draw a whisper piece from the bag, though

James huffed and said he hated to see such foolishness. Alexander chaffed him to quietness, though. He always could. And then he drew to please me. Rad came, that is the cartwheel, but twas back-facing, so his path be set hard and must be followed. There is naught else to be done. But I smiled when I put the pieces away, for the wheel will bring him here again.

20

I have done naught to deserve the trouble Grizel Mitchell have heaped on my head. She festered our few bickering words into a wild and overgrown malice. James be near off his head with fretting. He says such trouble be like a burn that dip under the ground and out of sight, but runs still and will come up again. I told him tis finished now and we have no more to fear. That with Mister Reid to speak for me, none will dare try to blacken my name again.

Minister Guthrie stopped me as I came out of Mister Reid's house. He said I must go with him to answer serious charges. That if I would go willing, he would not call the bailies. He be a kindly man, but he kept hold of my elbow as he spoke and his words stiffened my limbs with fear. Mister Reid saw it from his window. He could not have heard what was said, but I think my very stillness gave him disquiet. I still held sucked breath tight in my chest when he appeared and told the minister to bring me into the house.

What a knotted thread of mischance and zealous devil-seeking unravelled there. Guthrie had word from Forfar that Mitchell had gone to speak some business with a dozen others. One of those had long been suspected of cursing and scrying and when the Forfar Kirk Sessions questioned her neighbours, they found evidence enough to arrest her. It seem Mitchell spoke to some of the woman's friends and as the Tolbooth filled with one after t'other, her name was given. Tis always the way of it. A naming be enough. And she named me.

She said I had called up the great storm. That my chantings

had drawn all the winds of the world to Dundee. That fairies and kelpies were seen flying from my hand to sail away up the river to the sea. I laughed aloud. Mostly from the fear but also at hearing such storifying nonsense from a learned man's mouth. He did not laugh, though. Just said the worst was yet to come, for she had heard me foretell the wind would kill Dundee when it blew the harbour away.

I felt my face grow hot and fisted my hands, digging the nails deep and thinking only on that when he asked if I had summoned the wind. Even withal, I near laughed again but I caught Mister Reid's eye and knew he willed me to keep serious and say little. So I said I had not.

He asked if I had chanted spells and caused fairies and kelpies to fly from my hand into the river and out to the sea. I said I had not.

He asked if I had foretold the destruction of the harbour. I stayed silent

Mister Reid gave me a small smile to bring courage then poured wine for the man and told him there could be none in Dundee who had not known a storm was brewing. He had felt the betokening changes in the air himself. And the whole town knew what a poorly thing the harbour had been before. The shoremaster had fairly worn himself out warning that it would disappear into the river if naught was done. And without a harbour, Dundee was indeed a dead thing.

Guthrie nodded as though he saw the sense of it but then said he must act upon an accusation of summoning ill weather, and commanding fairies and kelpies besides. He could not leave these matters unquestioned. He must follow the law. Mister Reid asked what manner of educated man would give credence to women's foolish pratings. Guthrie nodded all wise under the weight of his words, and the hoping raised my feet off the floor and near squeezed the breath from me. But then he spoke again of his duty under the law and Mister Reid sent me to wait in the kitchen. I could see Guthrie did not like it, he feared I would run away, but he took Reid's word that I would wait as he bid.

No waiting was ever so long and so short together. All the life of the kitchen flowed back and forth before my eyes, but seeming far away. My ears were stopped with the fright, and the chatter and crash of busy maids sounded thick, as though haar-muffled. I thought on how I might seek Mitchell out, bring her before Guthrie and force her to tell how she had stood and listened to me speak to Margaret about that harbour until I sent her off. But then I knew I could not speak Margaret's name at all without visiting danger upon her innocent head. And once that thought was with me, it put me to thinking how I must get word to her of what Mitchell had said, for fear she was named too.

When I was called back, Guthrie had gone. Mister Reid said he thought he had brought the man to sense, but I must know he could do naught but follow his duty and put the matter to his fellow ministers, before the accusation might be recorded as no more than a wicked lie. Though it had taken all his arts and skills, he had got Guthrie to agree I might stay free while they spoke and pondered the law, so long as I did not run away. He said he had gave his word and I must not betray his trust in me.

I felt my knees tremble and sweat drenched my face. Mister Reid sat me down and put a glass in my hand. It shook like a palsied thing and I feared to drop it. When I steadied he had me tell all I know of Mitchell, all I thought might have caused her to name me. He listened close, questioning some small matter or another at times, but his manner was quiet and I grew bolder because of it. I spoke as natural as I would to James for I have done naught wrong. When I told him I wanted to bring her to Guthrie he said twas not likely she would manage the journey. Seemingly the witchfinders used the cashielaws and one of her legs was so crushed her watchers near vomited at the sight of it.

I sat long before I told James that night, too shamed to speak the words, though I cannot rightly say why even now. I felt myself branded an unclean thing, a creature to be reviled and spat upon. When at last I began to speak, I thought he would surely drop dead. His eyes bulged out and a deathly white ring appeared around his mouth. I whispered, for fear neighbours would hear, and because he do not hear well nowadays, he stayed quiet, listening close, and did not stop my words every half dozen. The whispering cleared a path through my fear-tangled thinking, for I must speak slow and careful and this calmed the sense of words that had grown huge and shrieking. And it gave me courage enough to go and see Margaret, once the darkness closed to hide me. I think I have never done a harder thing than look that woman in the eye and tell her she might do well not to say she knew me now. I could hardly bear to lose her friendship, but I knew good sense must keep her away from me.

She be braver than any man I know, for she asked if we had not grown like sisters now. And what manner of sister would deny kinship on the first breath of ill fate. Glad though I was, I warned her, twicefold, of all the trouble that might attend her loyalty, but she would hear no more of trouble. Indeed, she offered to speak with Mitchell's neighbours for me, the better to prepare me for what more questioning Guthrie and his like might devise. But I could never let her do that. She be too dear to me. So I made her promise to keep away from them altogether, and turn her head from me until I could tell her all was well.

Tis a three-week since last I saw Margaret but I will go tomorrow, for now I may hold my head up again. I need not fear James will lose all his business because of me. I need not hide from folk who cannot afford to be seen with a named one, because all of Dundee are named. I know I am glad to be free of it, yet the fear ran so deep I think I will never be rid of its memory. And James is marked with it. He be like an old man.

Mister Reid sent a maid to bring me to his house today. He said Guthrie spoke long with Scrymgeour and Rait, and ministers from the Forfar Sessions, and twas known now that Grizel

Mitchell called every name she ever knew during her trial. She called merchants, councilmen, the Provost, Daft Dougie who hauls creels of coal. She even called Great Michael, though it seem the witchfinder did not know ship from man. So they did not think it just nor fitting to proceed on the word of a woman so clearly out of her wits. I picture Grizel Mitchell now. She irked me sorely, but I could weep to think of what drove her few wits away.

21

I am lazy at my lifebook nowadays. Too long a time separate one piece from another and I forget that I meant it to say my days for the women yet to come. I picked it up today and saw I have not writ for months. I cannot think why. There be naught else to do on a Sunday. I do not mind so much sitting idle when the days be short and cold. The silence of the town do not seem to hang so heavy in the dark. But when the sun shine and the birdsong be loud, my feet itch to walk abroad. Tis no more than a yearning after forbidden pleasure. The minister said today all fancying and storifying was wickedness that drew our thinking from prayer and truth. I will make amends for my wickedness by placing a true thing here now, for no fancy could be droller.

Mister Reid have got himself the strangest device I ever saw. Tis two pieces of glass set in wires, with long hooks at the side. When he settle the thing on his nose, with a hook to each ear, the pieces sit before his eyes like clear pennies. He called them lenses and said they make words on a page bigger and easier on his eye. Tis sure the look of his eyes, all toadlike abulge, was not easy on mine, but he say tis a great fashion nowadays. I would not even have the price of the fine box he keep them in.

He paid me well for the word that Williamson have begun selling as though twas plack and penny day. Mister Reid like to hear such things so that he may buy and sell according. I have long known the game and if I had his money I might even best him at it. After, I went out towards Broughty, for there is naught so grand as walking far out from the town on a warm day, with the herb smell thick upon the breeze. I picked a fine bundle of papple and its blue be bonnier to behold than any of Mistress Reid's silks, I think. James be gouty again so I must bring more hegbeg than aught else. He will only take it well hid in a broth, though boiling draw much of its power. He would have it that eating raw herbage poison a man, though when we were first wed I ate a whole plateful to show him there be no harm to it. He said I might eat like a sheep if I pleased, but he would thank me to set good plain food, fit for a hungry man, before him.

Mhairi the Gifted, who was grandam to Effie, ate raw herbage near all her life. Her gift was the sight and she believed the herbage gave power to it. She was no more than a child when she was drawn to the leaves of she-holly that have no spikes. Tis said she slept with them beneath her head and they brought dreams to her of what was to come. Tis the holly dreams kept our line safe, for they warned her to flee before that Black Death, that was the worst pest ever known.

She went with her mother, who was Davina, and one sister. The only other sister who lived was already wed and her man would not leave, so those three went alone and walked as far away as they could. They followed the Don bank until they reached the Correen Hills and Mhairi knew they would be safe. She searched until she found a hole in the hill wall. Twas long and dry and not so cold as town folk might think, for earth and rock be warm, even in winter. Our women say the earth will always shield and shelter folk that know to respect it. So long as a fire go and dry bracken be plentiful, a hole in a hill make a fine house.

They stayed near three year, hungered oft times, too oft for her small sister to live. But all the while Mhairi kept the leaves beneath her head when she slept. Then at last she dreamed her farmtoun and all others in the land cried out for hands to plough and sow, so she told her mother twas time to return.

They were not welcomed at first. Folk wondered where these

leathern, string-shanked creatures came from. But it hardly mattered. The farmtoun was empty of the folk they had known. There was a laird's son, orphaned but not yet bearded, so desperate for hands he paid near any price they named. So Mhairi and Davina settled back to the land near Dyce that was home to much of our line. On four strips where they had left but one. None of our women would wish misfortune on other folk, but none would gainsay that misfortune for one may bring reward to another. So it was with our women.

Mhairi tilled and her mother spun. Davina was known for the softness of the cloth she made from the hegbeg. She could draw it fine and spin it to the thinnest thread. Tis a pity to know a skill that once lived be lost to our line.

Reid be fearsome aggrieved and I had not the strength nor the temper to spend long calming him. It seem I am to blame for not bringing him word that an incomer have filled a ship with weaponry to send south for the King's war with the Hollanders. Hard as I try, I cannot keep up with what business be done in every corner of this town. There are too many new folk, and I am grown too old to have easy discourse with young maidservants as I was used to do.

I could not think who Reid spoke of at first, though I know him now. His high colour and fattened eyes mark him as a man much drawn to the whisky and the wine, and his wife dress wilder and foreigner than others. But she may pick what she please when his ships bring in silk. Tis said he bring pictures back too, that show what manner of gowns the French wear. I had not thought to mark the man. There be so many like him. They grow fatter and we grow leaner, and they be further away from ordinary folk than foreigners nowadays.

Now I must set a watch at the Rattray house, for Reid fear him as a rival. I cannot think how to do it, and I cannot see why Reid would want it done so terrible keen, for it seem to me if silks come in and guns go out, all be well in the rich folks' world. And as if twere not bad enough, I must pay my watchers from my own purse again, for Reid be away and the mistress with him.

The fledgling lives still and I am strangely glad. When James brought it in, all broken from a stone throwed, I spoke sharp for his foolishness in not wringing its neck when he found it. Injured birds cannot endure long and tis a cruelty to leave a creature suffering. But James have turned so old and saddened these last months, I could not but try my best for him. He says he had a raven when he was a bairn and twas the finest companion he knew. He miss Alexander, I know, but I would give much nowadays to hear him speak to me so soft as he do to that bird. Young Wull says the business of the harbour be so slowed tis near corked just now, but there is no help for it. Better a skipper miss the tide than the pest come in on his vessel. He says most folk stand good-natured until their passes be marked, but there are some who would try to push all aside in their haste to be first ashore. It do no more than hinder them, if they did but know it. When David Smillie catch them at it he look so long over their passes he seem to sleep on his feet. Wull says no ship will go near the port of London now, for they have the worst pest ever known. They cannot even bury their dead for there are not carts nor graves enough.

I went to see Annie yesterday. How we laughed to see her bairns and their friends put soot to their faces for the guising. The Hallowmas now be but a small echo of the Samhain that was old long before our line began. But tis an echo withal.

In those times folk ended their year with a night of wildness, when the harvests were in but before the cold gripped. The Auld Guidman and all his imps flew about the land causing misdeed wherever they found good folk. So blameless wives got drunk and cursed, even lay with men not their own. And blameless, sober men jigged round and round, laughing and screaming at the sound of the moonlit fiddler. But so long as folk were guised, no man could look at another and know if he be neighbour or demon. And so long as food and drink got spilled upon the ground for the Guidman to share, he would take his mischief home at break of day and leave the land unblighted.

The Reids be back at last and what a tale they had to tell. They could not take ship when he wanted because the Danes have joined with the Dutch side in the war. Danish vessels cannot cross here and our vessels cannot put into port there. So they got themselves to the Faroes on a small fishing vessel, thence to Shetland and Dundee. Mister Reid said the adventuring made him feel like a lad again, though he must allow tis more comfortable in the remembering than the doing. But it seem Mistress Reid have no taste for adventuring at all, nor any toleration left for sight nor smell of fish. It suit the cook fine, for she wears that travelling gown now and the scales have left barely a mark on it.

There be no woman in this town blessed with a handsomer son. Alexander be grown so tall and broad, I scarce knew him when first he stood at the door. Tis a sadness to see him away again, but what a month we have had. We were all unbelieving at some of his tales, but he swore he told no lie. He says the lands in the east are so strange there is not one thing in them that do not surprise. The eastern folk do not even look like us. They are small and thin, with narrow eyes, and the men are not thick-whiskered like ours. Their garb is loose. Better for the fearsome heat, he says, than thick coats and tight breeks. And they eat with two sticks, yet can pick up their fish or meat as easy as we do with spoon or fork. He brought two pair as gift for James and we laughed so much in trying to get even one mouthful with them. I see now why those folk are thin.

But he brought a better gift for me. Tis a bag of seeds that he said are from black poppy. I have heard the name but I have never seen it, nor any herb with black flowers, indeed. Twill be a rare sight when they come up. I must think on how to get me a sheltered corner to plant them in the spring. Mayhaps I will go out to Davina's croft. She be bedridden now, poor soul, but her grandson's wife be a friendly creature and have a new bairn besides. It seem women in the east will tie a few of the seeds in cheesecloth and give it to their bairns to suck when new teeth push through. What lass would not care for my seedlings for the sake of a night's sleep? Twill be a fine thing if they thrive.

My poor man have outlived most of his friends and tis a sadness for him. He said Jaks be full of strangers nowadays. But Young Wull told me so long as James go in with the raven on his shoulder, he have no want of company. The men are never happier than when that bird creak slow down his arm to take a sup from his pot. Some will tempt him with a crumb or two of bannock and he favour them for a moment. But always he return to perch upon James's shoulder and survey the company, like a dour minister. He be wiser than most of them, too, for he fly swift and sure to his perch at the window each night and falter not at all. Tis not every man reach his bed so easy after a night at Jaks.

Reid be fearsome ill-humoured since his ship was pirated. It carried claret and now the French are joined against England twill scarce be possible to get wine. It seem there are near as many English pirating as fighting upon the sea these days. I listened to him rant against his misfortune and for the first time thought him foolish and unworthy. The loss of his ship grieve him less than knowing Rattray have sent a hundred barrels up to Aberdeen just last week. I care naught for their rivalry. My Alexander sail under a French flag and I fear for him.

22

A terrible shouting from James again tonight. The neighbours complain and I can say naught in our defence but that he is not himself. He do not listen to me, but ask the same question a dozen times over until I am near out of my wits with the aggravation. And he will not leave me be to write here nowadays. When the strangeness be upon him he fancy my pen draw demons down to the page. I thought he would burn my book t'other night, but I was too quick for him. He forgot all he had said and done not long after, but now I keep it well hid and take it out only when he sleep.

Tomorrow I will go out by the lands of Blackness for the buckies. The weather have been warm enough to bring them to ripeness early, I think. Twill be good to see Auld Donal again. I like his wily way of pretending feeble wits even while his eye glitter with sharp cunning and secret humour. I got my first crock from his still when Alexander was but three years. Twas my price for pushing his shoulder back in. He was not best pleased at first that I saw him take a jug from his grange, but his arm pained him greatly and he would not let me near him until he had took a cup or two. After, he could scarce believe I had done it so quick and sure and ever since, I have traded a crock of my cordial for one of his spirits.

Twas the first Helen of our line that watched the buckie wasps. She was born on a Midsummer Eve, when fairy folk and witches fly abroad. Some will take a newborn infant as plaything and keep it seven years if its mother do not take care to set lapper gowan to its head and feet. But some others, seeing the mother keep her infant safe with uncommon wisdom, will reward the woman by gifting the babe a tiny speck of their knowledge to use for good or ill. Tis that speck led Helen to the buckie wasps. She watched them build the galls on the fruit and thought to dry the white worms within. Naught drive worms from the belly quicker than dry buckie worm pounded to sand and put to hot ale.

Helen was born into warring and she said the fairies that gifted her flew on to the Bruce's camp and gifted his men the courage and strength to win proud victory next day. Folk have said ever since that when the sun go down on Midsummer Day the Burn of breid still run fou reid.

Warring rumble through all our line. It may roll and thunder about my Alexander's ship as I write here. Yet now I am near at the end of the women I can name, I see we have survived war and pest and hunger. Every manner of trouble.

I know as sure and certain thing our line will not die.

There be but one name left and mayhaps tis the most important.

The first Mhairi.

A strangeness mist her, for she left Helen no name of mother nor grandam. Tis not our women's way and I once asked Elspeth why. She said none could know now, but twas likely she came from fairy folk, for naught else could explain it.

Twas Mhairi's hand made the bowl of ivy wood that Elspeth gave to me. I use it still, though tis worn thin now from pounding herb. She cut it from a branch of the oldest ivy in the land, its stem a foot and a half thick at the base. Near it grew a holly and a roddin and our women say she cut a pestle from the one and a spoon from t'other, though they were lost to Grizelda's fire when the soldiers came. Tis fitting that her Mhairi's hand cut and fashioned their sisters.

Each tree protect from evil witchery but all three together bring uncommon power to what be mixed and pounded with them. Now, tis my belief the cures gain power additional from being made in Mhairi's bowl. The hands of all our women have polished it smooth and its inner shell be glossful with the juice of every herb and berry it ever held.

Now I have writ her here, I see the mist she carry about her. When I think on all our women, tis as though I see them too, though I will never know if what my mind see be true likeness. But I can make no picture of the first Mhairi. And though all our women have known that fashioning wax or clay may bring a lover to their hearth or put an enemy to his grave, none have known who first learnt it. That tell me Mhairi had knowledge and wisdom unnatural.

James be cruel tormented by some of the bairns hereabouts. They mean no more than mischief when they ape his hobble and make believe they chatter to a bird upon their shoulders. He would have laughed and chaffed them not long ago, but now he cannot abide their grinning mockery. Tis useless to tell him they can do him no harm. He rage and shout until he have no breath left. I fear he will drop dead in the street if he go on so.

Tis a blessing my Alexander come home oftener now and the money he bring be welcome indeed. I cannot get so much as I was used to do from the curing and Reid send me away with pennies where I got shillings before. I cannot understand it. I bring as much as I can and no different manner of scraps but they do not interest him so much these days.

I have took to giving James a measure of Mistress Reid's pleasure in his ale at day's end. Tis the only way he will sleep through the night without waking and wandering abroad. It seem a sly thing to do, but there be no help for it. T'other night I had half the neighbours at my door after he caught me at the whisper pieces. I had not heard him come up the stair and he did not come in the room at first but stood with his eye to a crack in the door, like a thief, watching me. When he saw what I did, he stormed in, shouting and screaming that he would not have me bring the Devil's work to his house. He swept the pieces to the floor, stamping in rage. He called me vile, unnatural creature. Said he repented the day he ever set eyes on me. All the while, Jak screeched and flapped about the room like a thing demented and twas not until I told James his bird would die of fright that he quieted, and I heard old Tam calling out to try to pacify him.

He stood in the door with half a dozen shoving from behind to get a better look. And that caused more shouting, from Tam this time, to be away to their beds and leave troubled folk in peace. Then he came in and spoke kind and soft to James until he saw his head nod in sleep. Tam is a good man, but too old for such botherments.

23

At last I may sit down with my book. I should not let disheartenment and weariness keep me from it. James be quieter than he was. Most nights he just sit silent, gazing at naught but the bright ghosts of times past that flit across his mind. Yet still I dare not bring it from the kist for fear he take another fit of raging. But Alexander have took him out now, so I have a fine long time to myself before I must get their dinner.

I have been thinking long days on what best to do about Margaret Coul. I am near certain of my path, yet tis a wise thing to set all down and look upon it writ, to see if the balance of good to bad still show the path clear.

I surmise she be another who would wear my shoes if she could. I saw her thrice in one morning, though I had gone up to the Reid house, then away across the town near as far as the Lady Well. I could swear she seek to know all I do with my days.

At first I could scarce find even one who know her, though there are so many new folk in the town now, tis no surprise. Then Young Annie said she is laundress and take linens from many of the houses. Now that would give her reason to be ever here and there and back again, all over the town. And tis true I have seen her with a laundry basket to her hip, though I heeded it not until lately. But she is not the one with her hands in the burn all day. They are not near raw and chapped enough for that.

So she fetch and carry for another. But her clothes be

unpatched and still true-coloured. Of finer cloth than washer-women wear. A woman so dressed would not likely take her own linen to the burn, leave alone run hither and yon for a laundress. So I suspicion the basket be no more than false device to let her go where she will about the town, seen by all but remarked by none.

I know her game well. But I was playing it long before she was yet born and I can beat her at it still.

Tis near April's end and I have not writ here since before Old Yool. That Jeannie Paterson vex me beyond all endurance. She held two ragged, pockmarked infants to my face today as if they might prove she had not my price. I told her she might find it easy enough to make payment if she only kept away from Old Mother Mackie's pot house. I cannot think why the bailies do not set the excise man to that woman. The spirit she sell be so poisonous tis likely to kill. James used to jest she distilled the dirty straw from the shambles and from the look of her customers, I would say tis more truth than jest.

Tis a terrible irksome way to make a living, though I cannot deny it turn five shillings into ten easy enough. Alexander look down in scorn upon moneylenders, like his father before him. I care not. Tis a business like any other. Tis only its secret nature that set it apart.

That Coul be at the curing now. Grace told me, though she must use words that seem innocent. No idle chatter be permitted in that house. She said only that Mistress Reid had no need of me now. But her eyes spoke loud. When I got to Reid's room twas clear he was not in good humour. He stood at the window, scarce heeding my words, until I set my price. Then he turned, right angered, and asked how I could think to expect money for such rubbish. He said he was aggrieved that what I bring from Rattray be not the smallest use in stopping the man besting him at half his business nowadays. He said he could not understand how I could fail him so after all he had done for me.

I was ready to spit with rage but made soothing voice, as I do with James oft times. I said I knew not what might be ado with him, that he could say I failed him when I have served him well since before Alexander was born, and he was twenty-four years October past. The man did not even turn to face me. Just puffed a small laugh as though my words mattered naught to him. 'Twas great paining to me. But I said only that I had served Mistress Reid as faithful friend too and though it seemed another brought her comfort now, none knew better than he what manner of sickness there was in his house when first I came. I told him he owed me much more than the few shillings I asked.

Still he did not turn, though I could see from the stiffness in his back he boiled with rage. He said naught. Just opened the window and threw my money into the street. I had to run like a thief down the stairs and out for fear it would be lost to me. 'Tis Margaret Coul have done all this.

I will destroy that woman.

I did not know I could miss my book so much. These last two months have been like a torturing without it. Alexander says I bring trouble upon myself. That I should hold my tongue instead of calling folk fool whenever the fancy take me.

I shouted.

Told him I was not made to hold my tongue at all and if I was minded, I could flay his ears with it.

My book would be lost altogether but for Young Annie. She was here when we heard the cry from the street that the Gillespie bairn was dead and the bailies must be brung for James. And Scrymgeour must be found. No lesser minister would serve, for decent folk would not have wizardry and evil live amongst them.

Such a screeching rabble I never saw and I spoke sharp at first when she cautioned me to give her my book, and aught else I held dear. 'Twas the anger at seeing my poor James, who know not whether he eat his dinner or his supper nowadays, called killer by a witless mob.

But she urged me, saying caution never lose as pride do, and because the shouting grew ever closer, I took her counsel and the book went out in my laundry basket, hid under a pile of linen, with the whisper pieces besides.

Tis as well she did for when the bailies came, they were four. Two to drag poor James along to the Tolbooth, and two to stick their busy fingers in every corner of my house.

Twice they came back in the days they held James, then twice again, days after Semple got him out. It seem they questioned right cunning, and he spoke long of a book. A big book.

Scrymgeour came with them at first, asking what book. Did I have any book? Why would my man speak of a book and naught else? What manner of book might an aged maltman keep?

I was sore tempted to ask what manner of man would question thus, all quick rattling, the better to affright and confuse. But I stayed my tongue and wore humble face. All the while the bailies scratched about my house where they would and I cursed them silent but strong for the pleasure they took in their work. I know one of them have a hoor every Saturday night, though in no ways could he know I have his measure.

Scrymgeour's manner was stern, but I saw to it he looked only upon an old woman. I told him we were God-fearing folk and I would speak naught but truth if only he would tell me, slow and careful, what he sought. Naught be easier than to flatter a man by seeming thirstful for his knowledge and pretending solemn admiration for his superior wisdom. Ministers be no different and so long as they behold the stamp of repentant sinner upon a face, they may be trusted to spare no words in showing that wisdom so fully as they may.

Scrymgeour spared no words. When at last his tongue was still I told him James likely spoke of the Good Book, for there was no man in Dundee keener to know all the lessons it might teach, as good Minister Semple could tell him. I said I could not count the many days my James walked out with that man and spoke of godly matters. And though oft times he could scarce recall his own name, my James never forgot his verses and chapters, and was never happier than when saying his prayers.

I am pleased to think Minister Scrymgeour got more holiness than he bargained for. But when the bailies found my cordial crocks, he said he would not have thought to find liquors in the house of a God-fearing man. So then I must press a cup upon them, chattering all the while that twas the best remedy for winter coughing, as surely their good wives would tell them. I doubted not they would feel the benefit in the morning, I said, and would be glad indeed to know if it was so.

The two bailies supped with pleasure and I smiled secret when they coughed long to gain a second cup. But Scrymgeour took naught. Said though the cordials and wines be tasteful to some, and not yet forbidden by the Church, he was pleased to keep his God-given body free of their dangerous fumes.

God help us all if the Church ban wine and liquors too. There would be no pleasures left to folk at all. If ever a man needed a drop or two to lighten his burden of fearful piety, tis him. His waxen cheek and dark-ringed eyes tell me he be not long for this world. He look so like a fresh corpse, tis a pity he will not permit his flesh a little fuming of buckie or bullister before he meet his maker. I cannot think such blackdusty grimness would enliven eternity and care not to meet him there.

After, he went back to worry my James about his bird. It seem Jak pecked at all who went in and out of the Tolbooth when James was there, and the fools listened to Marion Gillespie saying she never saw him without Jak, nor me with either. So twas clear to her that I am Jak.

There be no answer to such madness. When Semple came, he said James had told the ministers his spouse had bewitched him from the first day he set eyes on her. Poor daft man. Twas only old affection speaking but it took them two days to see it. So then I must go with Semple and Wull, who had spoke to the ministers already that James and me were of good upstanding character. And we must all three stand before them, with Jak hopping foot to foot on Semple's shoulder, to prove that if spouse were bewitcher and could change to bird at will, they could not be seen together.

Then it seem James said his spouse was uncommon clever, for she could read and write better than any he ever knew. So they sent the bailies again.

Such a breed. They be more rats than men, prying and picking and chewing their way into a life. Not questioning, after the manner of honourable, truth-seeking men.

But they have all the vanity of men. So when I wrote like a bairn upon their sclate, and pretended difficulty with reading their words, or understanding what they said, they believed me. For it did not fit with their puffing that an ugly old crone might do otherwise.

I would curse such vanity if I did not know its value well.

They sent a husk home. My poor James do not even hold his own spoon now. The only blessing is he sleep near all the time. He know not day from night so I may write free again, though I cannot leave him to go roaming and I think I might even give up my book to have him back as he was, huffing and shouting for his hat.

What terrible hardship and loss do old age bring.

I am tired beyond imagining of conniving stupid folk that crowd me, chattering wicked nonsense all the day long when they think I do not hear. I am counselled by Alexander to keep my tongue still if I cannot make it civil, though he know not the terrible vexations that lead me to rageful cursing.

Margaret and Young Annie say I should not fret when foolish simpletons run from James and Jak. Tis easy enough for them. They do not live day and night with a man who grow less of a man each day.

My James once stood proud in this town and fought to keep it safe. He once was welcomed as fine wit and sage at Jaks Tavern.

But now they turn him away as bad for business. Tis because of the whispering in the town. Tis because folk say Minister Semple died at my hand. Tis madness.

That good man died only because he was not afeared to go into the worst garrets to give comfort to dying folk. He followed me to places where even the bailies would not go unarmed.

I called him to the Buchans when I saw mother and bairn would not last the night. The small pox have taken ten in their close since the first days of August. There be no cure for it, though some live if they be strong enough and know to protect themselves when neighbours are afflicted.

I told him what ailed them before he went, and made a bunch of herb and aiten for him to carry. And I had set more to burn in the room, for the cleansing fumes, but it availed him naught. Tis my surmise he carried the sickness already, for I know he had closed the eyes of Jonet Miller two nights before. But at his funeral, folk kept away from us, so far as they were able in that crowd.

Twas then the whispering began.

Margaret Coul did not even whisper. The hussy spoke not to me, but loud enough that I might hear. Said twas strange indeed that so much death attended Grissel Jaffray's healing. That poor Minister Semple had paid a terrible price for befriending her.

Her face was all downcast in pretended sorrow, but her eyes showed the joy she took in her malice. She near licked her lips with pleasure, and the two matrons she spoke to chewed theirs, all relishful and nodding all the while.

Those fools would have nodded if she told them her face was green. She never cast a glance at me, though the eyes of her two cringelings flickered never-ending between us. I care not what that woman say of me. But when she said mayhaps my James paid worse price than Semple, for he yet breathed, though he be only half alive, I grew fearsome angry. I shouted she should not speak such wickedness about a poor harmless old man.

She turned then, all mocking surprise, and looked long at

me, up and down, up and down, saying not one word. Then she turned away again to speak of James being took. Said twas well known the provers did not always seek malignity where it truly lived.

There was no need for me to shout then. A silence dropped so hard into our midst it stopped her mouth and widened all eyes with fear.

I did naught but stare long and deep, silent cursing her and all her line. She knew what I did. I saw it writ across her face. Then I moved close and whispered in her ear that she should watch her words, lest they draw Grissel Jaffray's ire. Still she said naught and I went back to stand by my James, staring, staring, staring, until she could suffer it no longer and turned away with small laugh and busy chatter.

Scrymgeour and Rait stood at the Howff gate with Mistress Semple and her family. As we passed, Rait told me I would do him a great obligement by calling at the manse at twelve of the knock. I was minded not to go, for I wanted naught more than to get home, but Margaret Ramsay counselled twas safer to hear obeyment where obligement had been said. I knew she spoke truth, though tis an endless aggravation to me to take counsel where once I was used to give it myself.

24

I only wish I had thought to buy my own scraps sooner. Tis a profitable game to learn who be at the hooring or cock-fighting when their fine wives believe them to be at council or Presbytery business. Tis a real pleasure to me to walk past one of Dundee's finest and see him turn his eye from me, knowing he have bought my silence but not knowing how long. I like to sense the fear as I sense upcoming storms. It pay a little what this town owe to James, and to me if truth be told, for twas none other put an end to Montrose.

If Dundee folk but knew, they would thank me, not scorn me.

Fools.

Margaret Coul will end badly. I have seen to that. And her name will be forgot. I have seen to that too. A coal spurted the waxen to the floor at first, but it flared well when I threw it back.

Reid would not hear me when first I went with news of her game. Said I had better away and see to my poor James. So I went again. And still he would not hear me. The third time, he would not even see me. He left word with Grace that I was not welcome in his house. She did not like to say it for fear of my rage, and for her remembrance of old favours and I saw that, so I did not pour scorn upon her head. Tis not her fault she must work for such a man. I did it myself for years.

But I would not be forgot so. I wanted to watch Reid close when I told him what I knew of his new favourite. I wanted to see his face struggle to hide the wounding to his pride. I wanted to stand and stare and show him what he lost when he abandoned me.

So I watched and waited, garnering more scraps each day until yesterday, when I stopped him as he crossed the Market Gait on his way to the shore.

He tried not to see me, but I stride as long as he and stand near as tall so even as he hurried along, I asked if he would not wish to know why Mister Rattray still bested him. He checked his step once only then strode on, saying naught and pretending he knew me not. So then I said twas well known one Margaret Coul was oftener in the Rattray house than its mistress might wish. What might such familiar favourite not hear, I asked. And to stay favoured, what might not say?

Twas such a pleasure to see the import of my words battle with his show-naught face.

Young Annie is dead. Dropped like a stone to the floor not a moment after she had set the dinner before Wull. There be no reason for it. She was as hale as any woman I ever knew. Tis as though my own lass is gone.

I hear her laughter through ears half-stopped and see with eyes turned inward every turn of her head, every prideful wink to me at her bairns' droll chatterings. Tis past bearing.

Wull be like a shadow of the man he was. Tis a blessing the bairns are growed enough to see to themselves but still they are lost without their mother. Good Margaret step in now and then to see to them. She said the youngest was taunted in the street that her mother was took by witches. The little lass had to be lifted up out of a tangle of flailing arms and kicking feet, so staunch did she defend her mother. Bairns be ever ready to treat their playmates cruel, but those words were not the bairns' own. They heard their parents speak them.

Margaret be afeared for me now. She would go to Rait and tell him of the mischief being said against me. She think it have gone too far and must be curbed now. She would have me go to Reid too, for he be known in Dundee and if he spoke for me once, he will surely do it again.

I told her I would not waste my time. I care not what folk think of me now. She was sore vexed and she be the only friend I have left in the world, but I can do naught about that. She must stay vexed if she will not hear twas my sharp wits got rid of Scrymgeour and the bailies before, and can do it again if needs must. But there will be no need. They saw they made fools of themselves when they took my James. Tis not likely they would do it a second time. And though I would not say as much to Margaret, I know Bailie MacKenzie will do aught he can to stay clear of me, for fear I tell the minister of his hooring and gaming.

I look back on all my women, from Elspeth to the first Mhairi and I am proud to hold all their wit and wisdom in my heritage. And then I think upon the likes of MacKenzie and Reid, the ministers, the councilmen. They are held in high esteeming for no reason but that folk believe they must reverence their power and wealth. I see that any one of our women had power enough to best them all. How then could I fail?

Alexander was here for a day and a night. I had not expected him so soon but I had enough in my purse, even before he filled it, to put a fine fat hen to the pot. Twas a grand way to honour the day of his birth and it livened James most surprising. He was near as bright as he was used to be, and even walked to the shore with me to see Alexander away. It put us both in good heart. He will return not long after Hallowmas and that be only a week away.

I have not laughed so much in years. Coul stopped me in Over Gait, not far from the Reid house. Tis clear she think I work for them again and it pleased me most particular to leave her surmise undenied.

She said she would know why I had caused Reid to get rid of her. I said naught at all, just smiled a little and pretended surprise. Twas grand to anger her for all the aggravation she have caused me. The more I stood still and silent-smiling, the worse she got. She pointed her finger close up to my face and all the while, she chattered and hissed. I did not flinch. When her spit wet my lips I licked them long, and smiled the more, as though I tasted the finest wine.

At first folk passed to either side of us with no more than questing glance. But the more I fuelled her rage, the louder she got and twas not long before a knot gathered about us.

Two that seemed known to her came by. One skittered up, bright-lit with malice, not even waiting to hear what was ado before joining her midden-mouthed words to Coul's. The other lumpered slow behind then stood hard by, slack-jawed and peering close at me with the dull gaze of the mouth-breathing simpleton.

What a grand sight they made. The one like a codfish, t'other like a ferret. And Coul capering between the two like a demented hen.

But I could not enjoy it long before I spied two bailie hats nodding through the press of folk. Coul did not hearken to them at first and twas not until I smiled wide to see MacKenzie stop behind her that she ceased her vile threats. I bid him respectful good day, then told him I had said not one word to these women, yet they stood abusing me in the street. And I would be obliged if he would see them on their way.

He turned this way and that, asking folk if I spoke truth and I heard a voice or two agree that I did.

Margaret Coul began again, but was told sharp enough to keep her tongue still and her feet moving to home. She must obey, of course, but as she passed me she spat again and hissed loud that she would put an end to me.

I laughed full in her face at remembrance of the waxen running in my fire.

*C*harles, be the grace of God, etc. Forasmuch as Grissell Jaffray, spous to James Biuchard, maltman in Dundy, and prisoner in the tolbuith of the said burgh, is apprehended as suspect guilty of the horrid cryme of witchcraft, and to the effect justice may be done upon her conform to the lawes of this our realme, wee, with advyse of the Lords of our Privy Councill, doe hereby make and constitut John Tarbet, provost of Dundee; Jon Kinloch, dean of guild; Fothringham of Poury, Graham of Monorgran, Mister Patrick Zeaman of Dryburgh, Sir Alexander Wedderburn of Blacknes, John Wedderburn, Fiar thereof, or any three of them, to be our justices in that part, with power to them to affix and hold courtes, creat clerks, etc., and in the said courtes to call the said Grissell Jaffray and to putt her to the tryall and knowledge of ane assyse, and, if be her oune confession, without any sort of tortur or other indirect meanes used, it shall be found she hath renunced her baptisme, entered into paction with the devell or otherwayes that malifices be legally proven against her, that then an no otherwyse they cause the sentence of death to be execut upon her conform to the lawes of this realme; and generally, etc. – Subscribitur, Rothes, Cancell; Marshall; Erroll; Atholl; Dumfreice; Kelly; Airley; Weymes; Kincardin; Belheaven.

Commission for the trial of Grissell Jaffray, prisoner in the Tolbooth of Dundee under the charge of witchcraft, 11th November 1669

Register of the Privy Seal, Third Series, Volume 3, Page 91, Case Number 1859

(The National Archives of Scotland : PC1/40 p283)

Dundie, the twentie thrid day of November 1669 yeares convenit.

Anent such as were delated for witchcraft The ministers having alswa reprsented to the Counsell that Grissel Jaffray witch at her execution did delate severall persounis as being guiltie of witchcraft to them And therefore desyred that for their exoneration soume course mycht be taken against those delated The Counsell in order thereunto therfore nominats the provest the present baillies the old baillies deane of gild & uthers to meet with the ministers & to Commune with them on the said matter and to considder of the best wayes may be takin with the delated.

Taken from Dundee Council Book no VI 1669–1707
Dundee City Archives

Glossary of Terms

Aiten	Juniper
Auld Guidman	Satan
Barrikits	Rough tents made of bowed saplings
Braboner	Weaver – from *Brabanter*
Bullister	Sloe
Drookit	Drenched
Dwale	Deadly Nightshade
Foalfoot	Lesser Celandine
Foose	Houseleek
Great Michael	Star battleship of James IV's navy
Hegbeg	Nettle
Kist	Chest
Knock	Town Clock
Lady Day	Feast of the Annunciation, celebrated 25th March
Lapper Gowan	Marsh Marigold
Lippy	One quarter peck
Luckenbooths	Locked market stalls
Old Blearie	Robert II 'The Steward'
Papple	Cornflower
Plack and Penny Day	Day after market, when leftover goods sold cheaply
Poisonberry	Woody Nightshade
Ragweed	Ragwort
Reddsman	Municipal Refuse Collector

Regrate	Hoarding for later re-sale at unreasonable profit
Reisted	Smoke-dried
Roddin	Rowan
Sclate	Slate
Sneeshing	Snuff
Wilfire	Lesser Spearwort
Witch's Thimble	Foxglove